"This must be some kind of bad dream."

Kate shook her head slowly in disbelief.

"It's real enough, Kate," he said. "Just resign yourself to it."

"What kind of man are you, Greg?"

"The kind who gets his own way!" His voice was as clipped and cold as the steely eyes regarding her.

"And now there's nothing to stop you, is there?"

He hesitated, breathing deeply. "One thing. There is one thing which would stop me, Kate." He spoke slowly, as he moved closer to cup her face in his hands. "Look at me, Kate! Look me in the eye and tell me you don't want me! Then I'll let you go. Tell me, Kate."

It should have been easy. Kate felt the lie rise to her lips, but as she opened her mouth, the falsehood stuck in her throat....

English author **WENDY PRENTICE** lives with her husband and three sons in Worcestershire, only half an hour's drive to Stratford-upon-Avon, where she can indulge in a rediscovered passion for Shakespeare. While her husband loves long walks, fishing and motorbikes, she prefers a comfy chair and a good book. She gave up her job at the Home Office when her children started arriving, and answered a call from Mills & Boon for new authors. Wendy says one of the greatest moments in her life was walking into a local bookshop and seeing her very own book on the shelves.

WENDY PRENTICE

conditional surrender

Harlequin Books

TORONTO • NEW YORK • LONDON
AMSTERDAM • PARIS • SYDNEY • HAMBURG
STOCKHOLM • ATHENS • TOKYO • MILAN

Harlequin Presents first edition February 1991
ISBN 0-373-11342-0

Original hardcover edition published in 1989
by Mills & Boon Limited

CONDITIONAL SURRENDER

CHAPTER ONE

'IF YOU don't take your hands off me this instant, Toby
Marchant, I will make damn sure you don't feel the urge to go
near another female for months to come!'

Toby Marchant jumped back in some surprise. He was a
subscriber to the myth that a redhead's temper was surpassed
only by her passion, but his smooth good looks and
superficially charming manner had insulated him from the
reality that temper was the only form of passion he would ever
receive from Kate McNaught! He was certainly not ready to
come to terms with the fact that he was being turned down for
the very first time in his life.

'My apologies, Miss McNaught!' he sneered sulkily. 'I
should have remembered you have other—more important—fish to fry!'

Almond-shaped green eyes narrowed with a dangerously
calm glint Toby Marchant was too insensitive to recognise.

'I think you had better explain that remark.' It had been a
long, long time since Kate had lost her temper quite so
thoroughly. Anyone who knew her well would have run a mile
from her deceptively calm features and soft, dulcet voice.

'Come off it, Katy!' The unfamiliar diminutive grated
intolerably on her already taut nerves. 'You may have the rest
of the office block believing you're a frigid little prude, but you
and I know better, don't we?' A nasty leer distorted his too
handsome face.

'Do we, indeed?' Kate's green eyes began to glow like a cat's
as it was about to pounce, but his conceit made him miss the
all too clear warning signals.

'No skin off my nose if Courtney wants exclusive rights,' he
continued with blatant disregard for his health. 'I'll still be
around when his interest fades. Funny, though, I wouldn't
have said you were his type at all . . .'

Crack! Toby Marchant's head very nearly parted company with his neck with the force of Kate's blow.

'And if you don't want a black eye to add to your bruised jaw and over-inflated ego, I suggest you get out of my office right now, and take your filthy mind with you!'

'You little bitch!' He caught her wrists in a painful grip. 'No one punches me on the jaw and gets away with it!'

'Then you would be well advised to act on my secretary's suggestion!'

They turned as one as the cold, harsh tones reached them from the doorway. Kate would have screamed in frustration had she not been so mortified. How many more things could possibly go wrong in one day?

'Mr Courtney!' Toby Marchant was the first to recover and he hurriedly stammered his excuses. 'A personal argument, I'm afraid, sir.' His feeble smile faltered as he met the derisive gaze of his employer. 'It got a bit out of hand.'

'So I saw.' Gregory Courtney's long figure left its lounging position in the doorway and he moved towards them. 'I believe you owe my secretary an apology, Marchant.'

'I—I . . .' Toby Marchant's mouth was opening and closing like that of a fish. 'I'm sorry, Kate.' He turned and smiled with complete insincerity. 'But you did provoke me, you know,' he added with malice.

Kate was literally speechless with rage. Her green eyes sparkled dangerously, but before she could formulate her attack, Gregory Courtney, that most improbable of white knights, intervened again.

'I should warn you, Marchant, I heard a great deal more than you obviously believe I did,' he drawled with a witheringly contemptuous glance from his steely grey eyes. 'I will not tolerate my staff being subjected to sexual harassment.' Toby Marchant flushed uncomfortably, turned on his heel and made to leave the office, but he was halted by Gregory Courtney's further warning. 'And Marchant—if I hear any more rumours circulating about Miss McNaught and myself, I will know from whom they originated. Do I make myself clear?' One look at those hard grey eyes and Toby Marchant got the message. He nodded jerkily, and fled.

Kate heaved a sigh of relief that the distasteful scene was over. Loss of temper left her so drained of energy, and heaven only knew, she needed every ounce of energy she could muster to simply get through the day. And what a day it had been so far! A row with her father, a row with Toby Marchant, and now—with Gregory Courtney?

'No apology from you, Miss McNaught?' His low mocking tone and slightly amused glance caught the remains of her ambivalent mood. She drew herself up to her full sixty-six inches to look haughtily down her daintily freckled nose.

'I have nothing to apologise for, Mr Courtney,' she murmured primly, not quite meeting his eyes.

'Losing your temper in my time?' he suggested mildly, an amused quirk to his eyebrow. Those eyebrows, Kate had discovered long ago, were the best guide to his mood. The lower and straighter they were, the less approachable he became. One up, one down meant crossing your fingers for an extra edge. Kate crossed her fingers behind her back.

'I was born with my temper, Mr Courtney. There's very little I can do about it once it starts to blow.' She pulled a face, figuring she had burnt her bridges long ago. 'I've tried everything, believe me!'

She was subjected to a long, thoughtful stare from beneath his preposterously long lashes, the only hint of softness his hard face possessed. Kate shifted uncomfortably. He had the ability to make one feel like an object under a microscope. And she knew only too well what he would see.

Her oval face was framed by a mass of shoulder-length wavy red hair. She would have liked to be able to call the shade auburn, but in all honesty she had to settle for carrot. Fortunately, its thickness allowed her to bring some measure of control to bear, but in all the furore before she left home this morning she had only had time to tie it in a ponytail with a piece of black velvet ribbon. Knowing this had the—to her—unfortunate effect of taking about seven years off her twenty-three did little to boost her sagging confidence. Her eyes, her best feature, some said, were clear green. When she was tired, as now, they gave a translucent effect. They were tilted slightly at the corners, giving her a faint air of mysticism.

Although, to be fair, she was unaware of this, just as she had no idea how her generous mouth appeared softly sensuous to even the least discerning of men.

Kate was, though, justly proud of her figure. Not that she watched her diet too carefully—her mother was too good a cook for that! But the severely cut dark green two-piece suit she was wearing did little to hide her slender curves from Gregory Courtney's too knowledgeable eyes.

As she had feared, a deep flush, the curse of her life, spread up over her high cheekbones as she was pinned to the spot. Gregory Courtney had done this before, and mostly Kate had countered with an equally assessing roaming gaze of her own. But her self-possession, already so greatly diminished as to be irretrievable, was scattered to the four winds as he mentally stripped every item of clothing off her.

It wouldn't be so bad, she thought fatalistically, if I could only be sure he liked what he saw!

Suddenly their glances collided and locked. Kate's lashes quickly fanned down to hide the confusion she felt at what she had seen in his fixed regard. Just as suddenly, he appeared to tire of the game. Glancing at his watch, he stood and turned towards his office, his voice uninterested as he drawled, 'I would like you to lunch with me today, Miss McNaught. Be ready in fifteen minutes.'

Kate quickly cleared her desk and ran to the cloakroom to effect running repairs to her make-up. Lunching with her boss was no novelty. He would take her out at least once a week, mainly, she had decided long ago, to pick her brains about the various personalities they had to deal with. He did, she knew, appreciate her sharp perceptive abilities, and had even been known to take her advice on occasions, especially where union matters were concerned.

Kate had worked for Gregory Courtney for two years now, and in that time had learnt to respect his immense drive and business acumen. On the frequent occasions when they had worked long into the night to complete negotiations, never once had he showed signs of tiring, his mind as sharp as at the start of the day, when everyone else, Kate included, would be near to exhaustion. He had a great dislike of compromise, which could have made dealing with the several unions involved in his business rather fraught, were it not for his willingness to pay the highest rates for the standard of work he demanded. As yet, there had been no serious confrontations. Conditions of work were of the highest possible standard.

At only thirty-four, Gregory Courtney had the reputation of something akin to a Midas figure. It was only those working closest with him who realised just how hard he had worked for his present position in life. He had started with nothing, educating himself as best he could while working all hours. As soon as he had raised the capital, he bought his way into a small electronics business, eventually taking over as the owner lost interest. Gradually the business began to expand under his leadership, growing to its present multi-national status.

Kate had been aghast when she had first learned that she was to be his secretary. She had been quite comfortably ensconced in the Midlands Regional Office, when it had been decided to relocate the company's headquarters from London to the Midlands due to more favourable rating subsidies. Kate had been deputising for the secretary of the regional supervisor, and had thus been seconded when Gregory Courtney first arrived. Much to the chagrin of her former boss and Gregory Courtney's former secretary, he had decided to keep her. Somewhat to her surprise, she found she actually thrived on the challenge. He had been very patient with her in those first few weeks until she had found her feet. Her willingness to work hard and long hours without watching the clock had not gone unappreciated in her salary, and, over the months, he had trusted her with ever-growing responsibilities, until she was now more of a personal assistant than a secretary.

He was a very exacting employer, sometimes giving the impression of expecting too much from his workforce, particularly management. Any slacking or sloppiness was jumped on immediately. But one glance at the firm's balance sheet was enough to justify his high standards. And, Kate was fair-minded enough to admit, a word of praise was also forthcoming when deserved, always taking the recipient so much by surprise that their efforts were once more increased in the hopes of further recognition.

Kate herself was more than grateful for the opportunity to stretch her talents far beyond any self-imposed limits. Were it not for Gregory Courtney, there would have been no way she could even have aspired to her present position and high salary. Indeed, she had had no idea that such ambition was lying dormant in her until he brought it to life. Her work was far more satisfying to her now she knew herself to be a highly valued member of his team. She was no longer surprised, though, that Gregory Courtney had been the first to perceive her abilities enough to pluck her from the depths of the typing pool. He had never been slow to recognise management potential, regardless of age or sex, and he had surrounded himself with a team whose talents and personalities combined with his own to form one of the most forward-looking industries in the country.

No one, though, was ever in doubt about who was the boss. Not that he flaunted his authority. He was always willing to listen, encouraging advice even from the shop floor on occasion. But, being an essentially private man, he tended to hold himself aloof from people on a more personal level. Kate, for instance, was probably as close to him as any other person in the company, but he had yet to call her by her Christian name. In fact, were it not for those assessing surveys he occasionally subjected her to, she would have assumed he would have been quite content to swap her for a computer!

The first time he had dissected her with those cold grey eyes had considerably alarmed her, filling her young mind with visions of being chased around the office by a sex maniac! Now she could only laugh at her immature fears. Gregory Courtney had never so much as laid a finger on her! And that was just as she liked it. He was way out of her league in every respect. No—those dissecting surveys were more in the nature of unspoken punishment for real or imagined transgressions. It certainly had the effect of making her toe the line, although she had never seen him do it to other female employees.

And, Kate's incurably honest nature had to allow, it did make her feel rather good to be seen in his company. He had a presence which compulsively drew eyes towards him, especially those of the feminine persuasion. Kate had lost count of the many metaphorical daggers she had felt in her back from envious female eyes. Gregory Courtney ignored them altogether, if he even noticed them. His life away from the office was a closed book to her. She had never been requested to dispatch flowers and suchlike as other secretaries were. And he very seldom received private phone calls. That there were women, Kate had never doubted—his was too dynamic and compelling a personality for there not to be a woman in the picture somewhere. Although that was pure conjecture on Kate's part, as they were certainly never allowed to interfere in his business life.

She glanced at her watch and smothered a shriek, impatient with herself for standing wasting time on idle thoughts. When Gregory Courtney said fifteen minutes that was exactly what he meant!

She felt a momentary thrill at the sight of her employer leaning over her desk. It was something that had happened at odd times before and she had never quite identified it. It was something she tucked into the back of her mind until the next time it happened.

He looked up now as he heard her approach. He was of a tall, powerful build, radiating the impression of leashed athletic strength. He had dark, almost black hair, cut short, a lock of which was wont to fall forward across his lean forehead, giving rise to his habitual gesture of raking his fingers through it. His eyes were steel-grey, razor-sharp under their hooded lids, and adding considerably to his normal expression of cool indifference. Deep grooves splayed out from either side of his nose to his mouth, a mouth which rarely quirked with amusement, unless it was slightly mocking. Not good-looking in the conventional sense, but extremely attractive none the less. Kate had often thought he would make an excellent poker player.

She flushed suddenly at the sight of his raised brows, realising that she had been caught staring.

'Sorry,' she muttered with attempted lightness. 'I seem to be miles away today.'

'Wishful thinking?' he drawled, gesturing towards the windows where the sun was shining brightly from a clear blue sky, a foretaste of the summer to come.

'Perhaps.' Her lips moved in the motion of a smile. 'Shall we go?'

'In a hurry, Miss McNaught?' he asked, a small amount of surprise in his deep voice. Kate was in the habit of following rather than issuing instructions.

'I'm hungry.' She laughed suddenly, giving him a view of her perfect white teeth. 'I missed my breakfast this morning.'

'Indeed?' His eyes narrowed as if he found her statement of interest, but then he shrugged and led her out of the office, a courteous hand at her elbow.

Their usual restaurant was fortunately situated only a few hundred yards from the office block. A hovering waiter showed them to a booth immediately. Kate found the booths rather intimidating, leaving her in such close proximity to her companion, but as their conversations over lunch invariably concerned confidential business matters she found the choice understandable.

Gregory Courtney leaned back against the soft cushion of the buttress after they had ordered and surveyed her with hooded interest as her agitated fingers roamed the rim of her glass. She was still, in spite of her outward composure, suffering the after-effects of her scene with Toby Marchant.

'What do you think of Tom Nichols?' he asked suddenly, jolting Kate out of her introspection, for which she was grateful, although she would have preferred a different subject . . . discussing Tom Nichols would inevitably lead to thoughts of her father. However, she considered the question with her usual thoughtfulness. There was no surprise at having her opinion sought. Gregory Courtney was aware that she had known Tom Nichols a long time. He had just become one of the newest recruits to the local union executive.

'I think he'll play fair,' she said finally.

'You don't think he's out to draw blood? This is his first set of negotiations.'

'No, he's no hothead. Nor is he out to make a name for himself at any cost. He's—steady. He won't give anything away, mind . . .' Despite the track her thoughts were taking, she permitted a small smile to show. 'He's been too well trained for that. My father was his first teacher,' she added at his interrogative look.

'So that's where you get your understanding of union matters?' He nodded as if he had spent time pondering the question.

'I was brought up on it.' Kate's smile was more genuine this time as fond memories flooded back of hours spent debating with her father. They had put the world to rights so many times. If only . . .

'Your father is a shop steward, I gather?' He returned to the subject after they had been served.

'Not now,' her eyes clouded. 'He was a long-distance lorry driver. He was made redundant nearly three years ago.'

'Still not working?' The question was casually put, but despite her distraction, Kate sensed that her answer was in some way important to him. She shook her head warily, stilling the sudden crazy impulse to confide fully in him. Kate was always more than happy to share her joys, but problems were a different matter. Her natural reticence negated the impulse immediately and kept her replies short and to the point.

'What about your mother?'

Kate shrugged. 'She does a few hours a week cleaning offices.'

He grimaced. 'I imagine your father isn't too keen on that.'

'He hates it!' Kate answered vehemently and truthfully. Her father's natural pride at providing for his family had been severely undermined, as he was one of the older breed which firmly believed in the man's dominant role in life.

'And you have two young brothers, I believe?' Kate nodded, somewhat surprised. She could not recall mentioning Ian and Andy to him, and he was hardly the type to pore over family photographs! 'So, am I right in assuming it was money worries causing that little tantrum earlier, rather than something personal between you and Marchant?' His mouth twisted on the name. Kate gasped and pushed away her half-eaten lunch.

'You know perfectly well I don't go in for office relationships!' Her voice was a little huffy with indignation.

'But how on earth . . .?'

He grinned, her fluster obviously amusing him. 'Elementary, my dear Miss McNaught.' He took a sip of his wine. 'You've brushed off enough people with such cool disdain if they so much as hint at our—alleged relationship.'

Kate felt a painful flush spread over her face. She was all too conscious that her normal cool-headedness when dealing with her boss had totally deserted her. And, she suspected, he had only just started to take advantage of the fact.

'I didn't realise you'd heard the rumours.'

He shrugged off the matter. 'There are always rumours about a boss and his secretary.' He met her eyes, and added in a deliberately goading tone, 'Especially when the secretary in question is as young and beddable as you undoubtedly are!'

'Oh!' Kate's blush deepened as she gaped at him open-mouthed, shocked to the core by his offhand comment.

'Did you really imagine I hadn't noticed?' he asked gently, his deep voice slightly husky as his gaze dwelt on the swift rise and fall of her breasts. 'You rather intrigue me, you know, Kate.' Yet another surprise! Her eyes widened at his use of her Christian name. She really didn't think she could take any more today, but he continued, regardless. 'Today is the first time you've allowed that cool façade to slip. I was beginning to think it was a permanent fixture.'

'I could say the same about you!' she snapped, the heightened colour lending a sparkle to her cat's eyes.

'Action and reaction,' he shrugged. 'Now, about your problem . . .'

'I really don't think . . .'

'Greg, old chap! I was hoping to run into you here!'

Kate heaved a sigh of relief at the advent of Ron Millerchip, a bluff hearty man in his mid-fifties. He had been trying for months to get Courtney to speak at the local Chamber of Commerce.

Kate almost succumbed to a fit of the giggles as she noticed her employer's eyes glaze over. She had discovered very early on that Gregory Courtney hated the social side of business politics with a passion, delegating them whenever possible to his second-in-command Sam Goodis, an older man in his early fifties, whose plump gregarious wife, Marie, loved nothing more than entertaining. Kate had only met her on a couple of fleeting occasions, but had been struck immediately by her lively, outgoing personality. Sam, of course, she knew rather better.

Ron Millerchip had been unflagging in his efforts to contact Gregory Courtney. Kate had diverted him to Sam many times, but she now felt a perverse satisfaction from remaining adamantly silent in the face of her boss's narrow-eyed demand for rescue. It took a none too gentle kick on the shin from under the table to remind her that it was, after all, part of her duties to save her boss from such time-consuming irritations—even if he did deserve Ron Millerchip after that crack about her beddability. The nerve of him! She found it even more irritating to discover that the idea of him thinking of her in such a way was not altogether displeasing!

'I'm so sorry to interrupt, Mr Courtney . . .' Her voice poured honey in direct contrast to the message her eyes were delivering, 'I'm afraid you have a two-fifteen appointment . . .'

'Ah, yes. Thank you, Miss McNaught.' He stood up, obviously anxious to be on his way. 'Perhaps you could arrange something with Mr Millerchip,' he added absently, and heartlessly left her to it. Punishment, no doubt, Kate thought cynically, watching his retreating back.

'Now, Mr Millerchip . . .'

Kate returned to her office in a very fraught state of nerves, stuck out her tongue childishly at Gregory Courtney's door, and sank tiredly into her chair. She stared broodingly at the telephone for what seemed like hours, wondering whether or not to ring her mother. She felt too apathetic to concentrate on the usual pile of problems in her in-tray. She could never remember a time when she could not lose herself in her work. Then, startled, she almost jumped out of her skin when the phone rang, the discordant noise reverberating through the silence.

'Mr Courtney's office. May I help you?' she uttered automatically.

'Katherine? Is that you?'

'Yes, of course it's me, Mom.' There was only one person in the world who persisted in addressing her by her full name. 'I was just thinking about calling you. How is he?'

'Depressed, ashamed, guilty—and still as stubborn as a mule! You know your father, Katherine.' Alissa McNaught sounded very near to tears.

'I'm sorry, Mom. I know this is hard on you,' Kate sighed. 'I just wish I'd managed to keep my mouth shut.'

'You're no more capable of that than flying to the moon, once your temper is roused. Your father knows that, love.' Her mother's tone became dry. 'And you know he only gets so belligerent when he feels guilty. This row's been brewing for some time.'

'He's still set on it, then?' Kate asked without much hope.

'Oh, yes. More than ever.' Her mother sounded as tired as Kate felt. Their normally easy-going family life had been plunged into turmoil in the past few weeks, one argument following another with increasing regularity. It was taking a heavy toll on all of them. And Kate was stuck firmly in the middle. This morning's little episode had been magnified out of all proportion, but had forced Kate to understand that changing her father's mind was now probably next to impossible.

'Oh, Mom, I just don't know what to say any more.'

'I dare say we'll come through. I'll have to go, Kate—he'll be home in a minute. See you later, love.'

'Bye, Mom.'

Kate replaced the receiver and slumped tiredly on her desk, her head cradled in her arms. How could she have spoken to her father as she had? Losing her temper was no excuse, the thoughts must have been in her mind for her to have thrown them at him so carelessly. She could still see her mother's puzzled frown as she stared at the red print on the electricity bill. Her father's pale face told its own story. It had all come out then—how he had taken the money she had given him to pay the bill and blown the lot on a racing certainty. The fact that his horse had lost by only a short head was no consolation to Kate. The bill was for nearly sixty pounds and she simply had no reserves to call on.

Every month since her father had been made redundant,

Kate had quite cheerfully handed over her pay cheque, taking only enough for bus fares and sundry items like tights. She had felt no resentment. Her family had always pulled together in times of trouble. Even Ian had managed to get a paper round. But the upkeep of a four-bedroomed house, plus two permanently hungry and growing teenage brothers, had swallowed every penny. Her father's unemployment benefit barely covered the housekeeping without even touching the mortgage, rates, gas, electricity, phone and all the other seemingly hundreds of bills that had been pouring through the letterbox lately.

Kate's elderly Mini had been sold very early on, as had Callum McNaught's Maxi. Every month the boys needed some new item of clothing, they were growing so fast. And every week her father returned from the Job Centre, his shoulders slumped in defeat, his pride as head of the household diminishing slowly but surely, and Kate's thoughtless words this morning, instead of completing the process altogether, had instilled in him a determination to go ahead with the plans that were causing so much dissent.

And all morning the thought of that sixty pounds had weighed heavily on Kate's mind. She had to find the money from somewhere, but their savings were long gone. Thus far, they had avoided going into debt, but she suddenly felt they might now be at the start of that very slippery slope.

Her agitation increased a hundred-fold when she finally raised her head to find herself staring blindly into Gregory Courtney's impassive features.

'I'm—I'm sorry . . .' she stammered, horrified at being found in such a mortifying situation.

'Come into my office, Kate.' Said the spider to the fly, Kate added silently, rolling her eyes at his retreating figure.

She followed him listlessly, knowing she would have to proffer some sort of explanation for her unprecedented behaviour, but inwardly rebelling at the thought of betraying her father. It had, after all, taken his uncharacteristic action to make her realise just how desperate he was becoming to raise some money. He had known full well, without Kate's heated words, that this was not the way.

Courtney strode directly to the drinks cabinet concealed in the corner of the office and poured a measure of brandy into a glass.

'Drink this,' he ordered curtly.

'But I don't like . . .'

'Drink it!' The thread of impatience in his voice brooked no argument, and she tossed the amber fluid back with scant regard for its quality, wincing as it burnt the back of her throat.

He was perched on the end of his desk looking down at her by the time Kate's eyes cleared of their brandy-induced tears. She resolutely kept her gaze on his discreet silk tie as he began to question her in his clipped voice.

'Was I right in assuming it's money causing this—upset?'

'I . . .' Her tongue clove to the roof of her mouth.

'Don't prevaricate—just answer me. I don't need all the details, just a simple yes or no will suffice,' he rasped. She stole a glance at him through the veil of her lashes, but his granite-hard features gave nothing away—except that the left eyebrow seemed a little higher than the right. Perhaps she was in with a chance after all! He had discarded his suit jacket since lunch, and his shirt sleeves were rolled up to the elbows, showing the fine dark hairs on his muscular arms.

'Kate!'

'I—Yes.' She gave in resentfully. 'Well, partly anyway,' she added truthfully.

He expelled his breath on a long sigh. 'How much?' He strode to his jacket and removed his cheque book, his intentions plain. Kate's mouth went dry, but she managed to hold her head high and proud as she glared defiantly at his stony profile.

'Fifty-eight pounds, sixty-five pence.'

Unforgivably, he began to laugh. It really was the last straw on this most disastrous of days! Kate jumped instantly to her feet and stared wildly around her. There was a vague idea of a blunt instrument in the back of her mind! He strolled over and pushed her unceremoniously back into her chair, still with that hatefully amused quirk hovering around his mouth.

'Kate, I do apologise. But to think of you working

yourself up into such a state for a mere fifty-eight pounds . . .'

'It may be a mere fifty-eight pounds to you, Mr Courtney,' she bit out with pathetic dignity, 'but you do not have to count every penny coming into the house.'

The amusement left his features abruptly. 'No, I don't. Not any more.' His head tilted to one side as he surveyed her stormy expression. 'Have you considered that I may have been laughing in relief?' She regarded him suspiciously until he expanded, 'I was under the impression that I'd have to shell out a few hundred at the very least to restore you to your usual efficient state.'

Kate rubbed a hand over her face in a weary gesture which was becoming far too frequent these days. Her anger left her as suddenly as it had arrived. Gregory Courtney was only trying to help, after all.

'I can't take money from you, Mr Courtney.'

'You take money from me every month, and earn every penny,' he pointed out kindly, and with irrefutable logic. 'Consider it a bonus for keeping Millerchip off my back.' He extracted six ten-pound notes from his wallet and handed them to her. Kate stared at the notes blindly, a mist of tears clouding her vision. How she hated the necessity of taking them!

'Then thank you. I'll pay you back as soon as . . .'

'Don't be so ridiculous, Kate,' he snarled, his brows lowering to danger point. 'As you so rightly pointed out, it's a paltry sum to me these days.'

'But . . .'

He sighed heavily. He leaned over her chair, his hand sliding under her chin as he forced her to meet his searching scrutiny. Her uncertain eyes wavered and fell in the face of his piercing gaze. The tip of her pink tongue appeared to moisten her suddenly dry lips. Gregory Courtney did not miss the movement. His head lowered and his probing lips nibbled at the contours of hers, deepening the kiss as her lips parted on a gasp of surprise. He kissed her until her mouth quivered in involuntary response to his practised seduction. Then he drew back, straightening away from her.

'Consider your debt paid in full,' he said dismissively,

obviously unmoved by what, to Kate, had been a mind-blowing experience. 'Don't look so shattered, Kate. Worse things happen at office parties!'

She belatedly took her cue from him. 'Then thank you, Mr Courtney.' He smiled derisively at her polite little voice, causing her to add rashly, 'But it does make you think, doesn't it?'

'Mmm?' He looked up from the report he had just picked up to study, a puzzled frown drawing his brows together.

'Well, if I can get sixty pounds for a mere kiss . . .' She blushed painfully at the shout of laughter which greeted her words, and she rushed headlong out of his office before her runaway tongue ran her clean over the edge.

Gregory Courtney's laughter died the moment his office door clicked shut. Her taste had been even more intoxicating than he had imagined, he thought, resenting the fact, even as he acknowledged it.

It seemed the time had finally arrived . . .!

CHAPTER TWO

KATE had to forcibly stifle the yawn which was urging her to stretch out like a kitten, and turn her mind back to concentrating on the notes she was supposed to be taking. She had been sitting in the same position for over two hours now, and the conference room was growing stuffier by the minute. Normally she found Gregory Courtney's meetings interesting, if not fascinating. It was quite an education to witness at first hand his computer-like brain in operation.

The current round of wage negotiations had started the previous day. Sam Goodis was doing most of the talking, but the direction was being discreetly orchestrated by Gregory Courtney's infrequent contributions. Toby Marchant was sitting in for the first time as part of his management training.

He had been very subdued the past couple of days. Kate had wondered vaguely if her boss hadn't had a few strong words in private with him. Certainly the younger man had kept his distance from her. He had also very obviously been warned to keep his mouth firmly shut during this meeting. Kate had caught him biting his lip on many occasions, but he did not trouble to hide his condescension from the union team. A bad mistake.

He'll learn, though, Kate thought, as she recognised her father's training coming out so well in Tom Nichols.

'Could you just clarify that?' the youngish, stocky man was saying for the umpteenth time, causing Toby Marchant to roll his eyes in disgust as he totally misread Tom Nichols as a simpleton.

'You have to make them talk your own language, Kate,' her father had told her so many times. 'Keep things simple, basic. Don't ever be afraid to ask for explanations again and again for fear of appearing stupid. Don't let them blind you with figures. You want an agreement in plain, simple English with no room for loopholes—unless the loopholes are to your advantage, of course!'

And, by the time negotiations were completed, the unsuspecting employer was tied up in black and white, complete with signatures, having totally underestimated his opponent all the way along the line.

Sam, though, was showing no sign of impatience. Neither was Gregory Courtney. He was sitting, as poker-faced as ever, at the head of the conference table. From her position at his side, Kate was afforded a view of his uncompromising profile, and she wondered for the thousandth time just what made him tick.

Their relationship had altered subtly since their scene a few days before. Despite his effrontery in stealing that kiss, Kate felt she had been allowed a glimpse into the private side of Gregory Courtney, and had seen a much more human person than she had heretofore perceived.

He had continued to call her by her Christian name, a fact which had not gone unnoticed by Toby Marchant, although he knew better than to comment on it. And Kate was only now beginning to realise that she had been putting on an act with Gregory Courtney for the past two years, trying to fit into the cool efficient role she felt was expected of her.

The past few days had found her acting far more naturally towards him. Except when she remembered that kiss. It was a source of great irritation to her that the feel of his lips—so much softer than she had ever thought possible—had never entirely faded away. That apart, he had enabled her to prove her trust in her father by handing over the sixty pounds immediately upon her arrival home that evening. And that meant a great deal to her.

Although it had been many years since she had viewed her father as a cross between Superman and God, her love and respect for him were an integral part of her. Which was why she so hated the atmosphere currently pervading the McNaught household.

An uneasy truce was in place at the moment, but Kate could not shake off the awful presentiment that they were merely experiencing the eye of the storm; something confirmed a lot sooner than she expected by the flustered entrance a little while later of her deputy, Susan Henshaw, to tell Kate that her mother was on the telephone—sounding very upset.

Kate paled, looking automatically towards Gregory Courtney for permission to take the call. He rose immediately and helped her to her feet.

'Put the call through to my office, Miss Henshaw. Sam, I think it may be as well to adjourn these talks until after the weekend. Gentlemen?'

There were murmurs of assent around the table, but Kate was unaware of the periphery activity, of Tom Nichols and Sam Goodis' concerned glances and Toby Marchant's narrowed eyes resting on the hand propelling her through the door.

'Mom?' Kate could only hope she sounded a lot calmer than she felt.

'Oh, Katherine! I'm so sorry. I know you said you had a meeting, but . . .'

'It's OK. Just calm down, Mom, and tell me what's happened.'

'Your father, he's—he went to the bank this morning, to see about a second mortgage.'

Kate felt as though a giant hand was squeezing her chest—tight. 'And?'

'And he hasn't come back! It's nearly four o'clock now. He should have been home hours ago. And, Katherine, I found some adverts cut out of the paper—you know, those no-questions-asked loans?'

'Oh, glory!' Kate closed her eyes in despair. So he had finally cracked!

'Do you need to go home, Kate?'

Her boss's harsh but concerned voice pulled her together faster than a bucket of cold water. She looked up and nodded, unable to even think of hiding her anxiety, as she might have done only a few days ago. 'Then I'll take you.'

'But . . .'

'Don't argue, Kate!'

She spared him a grateful glance before reassuring her mother, 'I'll be there in about half an hour, Mom. Mr

Courtney is giving me a lift. Please try not to worry. Is Terry with you? What about the boys?'

'They're at the Baxters'. Terry is feeling awfully responsible, Katherine.'

'Well, tell him to make himself useful and put the kettle on. I'll be with you soon.'

Kate replaced the receiver and turned to thank Gregory Courtney, but he spoke quickly as if he had already anticipated and dismissed her thanks.

'I take it no one is actually hurt?'

'No, my father . . .' Kate cleared her throat and tried again. 'It's a long story,' she warned.

'Then we'll talk about it on the way.'

Kate strapped herself into the sumptuously comfortable front seat of his Mercedes and stretched back lazily, appreciating the luxury. She could not help the ironic imp of black humour touching her lips.

'Something amusing you?' Gregory Courtney asked with something of a snap as they drew out of the car park.

'No,' she exclaimed instantly. 'At least . . . Well, if you must know, I was simply thinking that this is much better than a number eleven bus—not that you'd know much about that!'

'Do you resent my wealth, Kate?' he asked quietly.

'No, I don't think so. Not consciously, anyway.' She grinned faintly at him as he took his eyes off the road for an instant. 'Seriously, though, I don't think it's your wealth I resent as such. After all, you've worked hard for everything you've got.'

'Thank you so much.' The dry note in his tone gave Kate the audacity to continue.

'It's what you do with that wealth which concerns me.' His features did not alter for a moment, then he threw her a surprised glance. The eyebrows were slanted downwards! 'Not that it's any of my business, of course.'

'I'm glad you realise it,' he snapped. 'Do go on, Kate—I'm fascinated.'

Kate doubted that! 'It's just—well, take this car, for instance . . .'

'Ah, the trappings, I see. Would you prefer me to trade it in for a bicycle? Is that more environmentally acceptable?'

She pulled a face at his sardonic inflection. 'I'd take a bet that after a ten-minute lecture from my father on the subject of foreign cars, you'd be happy to trade it for a Mini!'

She fell silent, wishing she had not mentioned her father, and let her eyes drift to her employer as he concentrated on the road. He showed no impatience at the heavy traffic. Kate liked that. She had been driven by too many foot-tapping men in the past. Gregory Courtney simply rested his strong hands on the steering wheel and waited. He had rather nice hands, she noted irrelevantly. Long, lean, sensitive fingers . . .

'So, are you going to tell me the problem, or do we have another round of Twenty Questions?' He spared her a cursory glance before turning his eyes back to the road. Their earlier exchange had restored some colour in her face at least, he thought, but heavy frown lines were still pleating her brow.

Eyeing him discreetly, Kate felt her reluctance to confide in him begin to drain away. He no longer appeared to be her imposing, emotionless boss, but more a concerned—friend? Well, that was going a little far, perhaps, but she did know there was no better person to advise her. Business-wise, his senses were acute. He was also totally objective, something Kate could not hope to be, torn as she was between her father's need to grab at the chance to restore his pride and her mother's fears for the family's security.

Slowly the words started forming, and before long, she felt the tremendous burden she had been carrying for weeks begin to lighten.

Almost four weeks ago, Alissa McNaught had opened her front door to find a smiling, suntanned Terry Walsh leaning on the doorbell, having newly returned from Australia.

The whole family had been thrilled to see him again. Although Ian and Andy were too young to remember him, Kate had been reminded non-stop of the days when she was a youngster, and her father and Terry had taken her on their long jaunts around the country when they worked together on car deliveries.

Callum had trained Terry, moulding the then enthusiastic but hot-headed youth in the discipline of long-distance driving.

Once he had saved Terry from certain dismissal; and Terry had never forgotten his old mentor.

Long hours on the road had a tendency to forge strong bonds between people, to make them open up to each other with surprising candour. Callum and Terry had shared many a pipe dream, but none more beckoning than starting their own haulage business.

Inevitably, the dreams had fizzled out as they have a habit of doing, and Callum and Terry went their separate ways, Callum to driving petrol tankers at the height of the oil boom, as Terry headed for Australia to make his fortune.

Which he had—a pittance to a man with Gregory Courtney's wealth, but a fortune none the less to Kate.

Enough to buy himself a truck and set himself up as a freelance haulage driver. Assuming Callum had received a fair amount in compensation on being made redundant, he'd invited the older man to join him.

Kate refrained from going into details to her boss, but it had been her father's union activities, coupled with his strong principles, which had manoeuvred him into his present position. His employers at the time had attempted to pay him off in an attempt to get him on their side, but, as Callum had later explained to Kate, 'I like to be able to sleep at night when I put my head on the pillow. I'd never again be able to do that if I were to sell my workmates down the river.'

And so they had let him go with scant recognition for all his years of service. Terry had understood immediately the position was explained to him. He was saddened that Callum would be unable to join him at present, but promised he would be the first man taken on when he was in a position to expand.

And that, Kate had thought, had been that. But for over two weeks Callum had brooded on his lost opportunity. His mood, generally mellow, became volatile. It had been an echo of the early days after he had been made redundant. The fear, the insecurity, the rage before, finally, acceptance of his fate. There was no acceptance now.

What none of the family had recognised until the last few days was Callum's desperation. Not until the day he had asked

Kate to sign away their home.

'It was signed over to me so I could claim the tax relief on the mortgage, you see,' Kate continued, almost oblivious of Gregory Courtney's presence by now in the relief of sharing the problem. 'They started buying the house over twenty years ago, so its value has increased immensely. But we're having difficulty finding the present mortgage payments. If there were to be a second mortgage too . . .' There was no need to go further. Instead she explained what had happened to precipitate her mother's urgent summons.

'The bank obviously refused to consider a second mortgage without my signature, so now he's approaching the loan sharks. It's not that I don't believe in my father's ability to make a go of it with Terry,' she was anxious that he should not misconstrue her misgivings, 'but it has to be a risk, doesn't it?' It was a hypothetical question. She did not expect or wait for a response. 'I'm not much of a gambler, I'm afraid.' She gave a slight smile. 'I still get panic attacks every year when the Grand National is run—and that's only for a five-pence bet—each way at that!

'It's just—I feel completely split down the middle. Either Mom loses the security of her home, or Dad loses the last chance to restore his pride as the head of the family.' Her voice quavered. 'It's—hard to watch a man be slowly stripped of the one thing to give him any dignity.'

A strange, painful expression crossed Gregory Courtney's hard features for a moment, a moment so fleeting it was lost before Kate could decipher it.

'Yes,' he agreed curtly, his voice harsh, 'I can understand that. I can also understand your reluctance to get into debt. I'm wary of debts myself, but . . . How old is your father?'

'Fifty-four.' Kate had no trouble deciphering his grimace this time. It must have been a look her father had seen a thousand times on his search for work.

'You'll probably find that's the main reason the bank turned him down. Just how long have you been supporting your family single-handedly?' he asked quietly, cornering her into a defensive position.

'We all do our share.'

'Sheath your claws, Kate,' he drawled, shooting her an amused though admiring glance. 'Believe me, I envy your father your loyalty. I'd be the last to attack it.' His mouth twisted a little as he said that, and suddenly Kate felt immensely curious for the first time about his background.

She knew so little about him personally that it had only been an innocently overheard conversation which had told her that he and Sam Goodis had been friends for considerably longer than she had realised.

Watching him now, Kate could almost see the wheels turning in his mind, though his concentration on the road did not waver for an instant. She would normally have felt embarrassed at having offloaded her problems in this way. A week ago she would not even have considered it. It was, perhaps, an indication of how very near the end of her tether she was that she had spoken so freely.

'What about Walsh?' Gregory Courtney asked some time later, once the heavy traffic was behind them. 'How old is he?'

Kate had to think about that for a moment. 'He must be—oh, early thirties, by now. He certainly has the drive and enthusiasm.'

'I see. And your father was to supply the experience?'

'Something like that,' Kate agreed, pointing out the next turning as they neared her home.

He parked the car immaculately in a space Kate would not have attempted to back her old Mini into. She looked up at him as she unbuckled her seat-belt, but before she could speak he was out of the car. He walked with such economical grace, she thought idly, thanking him as he helped her out.

She looked up at the house. A curtain twitched—a sure sign her mother was looking out for her—and Kate was suddenly unsure whether or not to invite Gregory Courtney to stay. For some strange reason, she was beginning to think of him as a sort of lucky mascot, as if his mere presence could set her world to rights in the blink of an eye. Until she thought, with horror, of the meeting she had dragged him from, the hundred and one things awaiting his attention in the office.

But once again he took the decision away from her by the simple expedient of placing a hand in the small of her back and ushering her unresisting body forwards. The door opened before they were half-way up the path, and Terry came out to greet them.

He was a tall man, almost as tall as Gregory Courtney, his hair as blond as Gregory's was dark, his sunny face again a direct contrast to her employer's remoteness, Kate thought as she performed introductions. Terry became friends with everyone he met, but his famous smile was sadly absent today.

'I'm sorry about this, princess!' he declared, draping a casual arm about her shoulders. He had called her princess for as long as she could remember. 'You must all be wishing I'd stayed in Australia—in fact, I'm thinking the same myself. He's back, love—turned up about ten minutes ago.' His blue eyes clouded. 'He's got forms from loan sharks all over the bloody Midlands! I think he's decided it's showdown time.'

'It's not your fault, Terry. You weren't to know,' Kate sighed, and led the way into the house.

The hall seemed to shrink in size as the two men entered, forcing her to see the house through Gregory Courtney's eyes. Not exactly the sort of place he would be used to, that was for sure. But, despite the slight shabbiness of her surroundings, Kate loved her home just as much as her mother did, right down to the faint fingermarks on the wallpaper. It was a haven to her, exuding the same unaffected welcome to all comers, be they Ian and Andy's schoolfriends or millionaire heads of multi-national companies—a 'take us as you find us' attitude Kate had practised all her life.

But the house, these days, also reflected a hint of the gloom which had pervaded since Terry's arrival. One look at her mother's face confirmed Kate's worst fears. Her father was obviously in one of his 'I'm the head of the household' sort of moods. The Women's Lib movement never had and never would make the slightest dent in Callum McNaught's way of thinking.

'Alissa McNaught—Gregory Courtney.' Kate tried to smooth her mother's agitation by reminding her of her manners. 'I've been explaining to Mr Courtney . . .'

'Oh, so you don't trust your dad's judgement these days? This is no one's business but ours, Kate . . .'

Kate whirled, stricken, as her father's voice, full of hurt pride and sheer pigheadedness, sounded behind her.

'Not at all, Mr McNaught,' Gregory Courtney stepped smoothly into the breach before Kate even had time to feel embarrassment at her father's attitude. 'Kate had the good sense to make use of my experience in these matters. There are any number of pitfalls ahead of you both . . .'

'If you think you can talk me out of it . . .'

'On the contrary, sir.' One eyebrow rose—and Callum relaxed. It was extraordinary, Kate thought, how charming Gregory Courtney could be when he put his mind to it. It had been a stroke of genius to add that touch of deference, even as he took complete control.

In no time at all, it seemed, Courtney, Callum and Terry were seated at the dining-room table, surrounded by a mountain of paper. Kate, of course, had witnessed such scenes before. But Alissa McNaught had never yet met a man capable of quieting her husband with one lift of an eyebrow.

'Well,' she muttered now, still a little shell-shocked, 'do you think . . .?'

Kate studied the closed door thoughtfully. 'What I think, Mom, is that Dad has finally met his match. Come on, I'm dying for a cup of tea!'

The next day, a Saturday, Kate spent mooning around the house, in a state of utter confusion concerning her feelings towards Gregory Courtney.

He had stayed for over three hours the previous evening, only leaving then because he had a business engagement that evening, as she had had to remind him.

Off the top of her head, Kate would have sworn there was no meeting ground between her father and her boss. But as the evening had progressed, she was forced to witness just how wrong she had been in her thinking.

Gregory Courtney had a very blunt 'take it or leave it' approach to business, something her father was not able to resent because he was equally blunt. And she knew she could trust her boss to tell her father straight out if the deal he and Terry had planned was feasible. He did so very much more.

For the first half hour or so, Kate had remained in the kitchen reassuring her mother, even though she was burning with curiosity.

Alissa McNaught was a very pretty woman still, though her grey hairs were now outnumbering the black. Her face was comparatively unlined, but her habitual smile had been absent for a while. Kate was glad to see it had not been lost altogether.

Kate always remembered vividly the day she had walked into the maternity hospital on her father's arm to see her brand new baby brother. Her mother had been sitting up in bed, her face radiant with the bloom of childbirth, looking impossibly young for someone who had just passed her fortieth birthday. The then nine-year-old Kate had almost burst with pride at seeing her mother look so beautiful.

Complications after Kate's birth had made Alissa believe it was impossible for her to conceive again. When what she had thought was an early menopause had turned out to be pregnancy, her joy was unconfined. She so enjoyed the ensuing months of pregnancy that Andy had made an appearance only eighteen months after Ian.

Kate had been awestruck the first time she had been allowed to pick up her squalling baby brother and soothe him to sleep. Even now she sometimes felt more like the boys' mother than a mere older sister. There was a very genuine affectionate bond between them, even when Kate was forced to act as referee.

Callum McNaught had aged considerably in the last twelve months. His hair was now iron-grey, his skin toughened to leather from the long days of driving open chassis in all weathers. But his brown eyes were still clear enough to recognise a man he could respect. Though Gregory Courtney's elevated position in life did not protect him from the ten-minute lecture Kate had warned him about. Entitled 'the thoughtlessness of people buying foreign cars, exporting jobs, etc, etc.', Kate had heard it a million times.

But Gregory Courtney took it all in his stride, had even had the courage to point out certain flaws in the argument, which Kate wished she could have thought of.

Alissa was captivated. Terry was impressed. Callum actually listened, and Kate? Kate was confused.

In three short hours, Gregory Courtney had disposed of a month of sheer misery and endless worry. He knew of a haulage firm which was entering receivership. He had been thinking, he said, of putting in a bid as he was dissatisfied with the present arrangements he had. But this, he felt, was better.

It would be an equal partnership for the three of them. He was willing for Terry and Callum to buy him out later if they were in a position to do so. Meanwhile, they were free to call upon his financial expertise at any time. He was also in a position to put lucrative contracts their way, but only, he stressed, if he was assured Callum and Terry could literally deliver the goods on time.

Terry was to put in his cash, Gregory Courtney would furnish Callum's loan at competitive interest rates, using the house deeds as collateral, and he would make up any shortfall himself.

Callum, contrary to the last, had, at first, demurred at taking Gregory Courtney's money, until Kate was summoned to pass judgement.

'Perhaps you can convince your father that my motives are rarely altruistic?' His voice held a sardonic inflection as he watched Kate swallow her excitement and to think of a diplomatic answer.

'Dad, if Mr Courtney thinks it a sound investment, then believe me, it is,' she managed finally.

'And if it isn't, I'm sure I can persuade the taxman to be kind to me. However,' he added, his face falling into sterner lines, 'I don't want either of you worrying about repayments until the business is paying. And before you mention the word "charity", Callum, this is pure selfishness on my part. I don't want Kate distracted from her duties as my assistant by money worries.'

'He believes in getting value for money,' Kate put in drily, speaking before she could think, then colouring faintly under the subject's mocking scrutiny.

'What else?' he agreed, his grey eyes warmer than Kate had ever seen them.

'But you don't even know us, Mr Courtney,' Alissa exclaimed suddenly, bewildered at the turn of events.

'I know your daughter, Mrs McNaught. Believe me, she is the only reference you need.'

And her mother, bristling with pride, had surprised Kate by becoming speechless, possibly for the very first time in her life!

And then it was left to Kate to see the family's benefactor to the door, all her gratitude suddenly submerged under a strange shyness.

'Have a good rest over the weekend, Kate,' he advised softly, seeing the signs of strain still evident in her tired eyes.

'Er—yes. Oh, Mr Courtney, I really don't know what to say . . .'

'As I believe you mentioned, Kate, had it not been a sound investment, I would not have become involved. As for the thanks I can see trembling on those delicious lips,' the timbre of his voice changed subtly, becoming lowly intimate, 'perhaps I may be permitted to receive them this way.'

And his head lowered.

It was nothing at all like the last time. Then, there had been a tentative quality to his kiss, as if he needed to test her reaction. Last time he had asked for a response. This time, he demanded nothing less. And when he had drained her lips dry, he turned and left, closing the door quietly behind him as Kate stood where he had left her, bemused, shaken—and not a little scared!

For so long she had looked upon him as a man apart from everyday feelings and emotions. He was not a man to give away much about himself. From the very little he had let drop, Kate received the impression that he did not think very much of the female gender at all. He was what her father would call 'a man's man'. But his kiss had told her he was no celibate.

And just why was he behaving so differently towards her? She could not believe he was after a brief office fling. That simply was not his style. And it certainly wasn't hers, as he must surely realise. Neither could it be that he had only just noticed that she was a more than passably attractive female. Her inner radar had homed in long ago on the fact that he found her easy on the eye. But why wait over two years to do anything about it?

Unless—unless he had been occupied elsewhere for all that

time?

At that thought, an alien pang of what she could only assume was jealousy shot straight through her. 'Oh, Kate, this has to stop right now before you make a complete idiot of yourself!' she muttered.

It would be the height of folly to fall for such a man, she told herself sternly. 'Two kisses and you're ready to turn it into the romance of the century!' She would revert to her normal cool brisk efficiency first thing Monday morning, she decided. Just as you've been trying to do all week since that first kiss, a little demon in the back of her mind whispered back. And Kate, as ever totally incapable of lying, especially to herself, had to allow that, unless she was very careful, she was in danger of succumbing to that favourite cliché of romance authors, the boss/secretary syndrome.

Fortunately for her peace of mind, Kate had been raised with more than a fair share of good common sense, which served to tame her wilder flights of fancy—of which Gregory Courtney had to be the paramount example!

He might have shown her the way to stretch her talents at work, but on a more intimate level—never! 'Just look at you now, Kate,' she castigated herself. 'Two kisses, a few leers and you're floundering! What if he decided to increase the pressure?' A cold nervous shudder traced the length of her spine at the thought. Then, her impish sense of humour coming to her aid, she chuckled at the sheer vanity of the idea of having a man such as Gregory Courtney chasing after her. The man was as much out of reach as Robert Redford!

Gratitude, she decided. That was why she felt so differently towards him. Gratitude, and perhaps a few errant hormones playing up! She had not had a date in months owing to pressure of work. She was probably a little hungry for male companionship—perfectly natural. She was only twenty-three, even if the burden of shouldering her family's monetary problems had matured her beyond her years. She would accept the very next date she was offered, she decided—so long as Toby Marchant was not the man involved! She did not count Terry's offer to take her for a drink later on. He was in the same category as her brothers.

Her mother was beginning preparations for tea when Kate was hailed by an urgent whisper from the garden.

'Kate! Quick!' Kate rushed out, expecting one of her brothers to have broken a leg at the very least. But it seemed the problem was easier to solve than that.

'Kate! It's my very best football! I didn't do it on purpose—honest!' Andy.

'Kate! You know Mom said she'd skin us alive if she found us climbing that tree!' Ian.

As younger brothers went, Kate had to admit that these two weren't bad. But there were times she could bang their heads together! Ian at fourteen and Andy at thirteen both had the rugged good looks of their father, although they had both passed him on the height charts. Kate resembled none of her family. She was believed to be a throwback to a great-great-grandmother.

'Aw, go on, Kate! I've never seen anyone climb a tree like you.' Andy.

'Forget it, Andy. I reckon she's getting too old for this lark.' Ian.

They walked away, whistling nonchalantly, knowing full well it simply was not in Kate to pass up such a challenge. She looked down at herself with resignation. Well, her shorts had certainly seen better days—mostly when she was a little thinner! And her halter top was not that special either. The years fell away from her as she took a careful survey around the garden. She wasn't too old to be skinned alive, either!

She was happily lost among the foliage when a sixth sense alerted her to danger. She peeped between the leaves, prepared to see her mother, then sank back in horror as the imperturbable Gregory Courtney came into view!

CHAPTER THREE

'I REFUSE to come down in front of an audience,' Kate announced stoically, thankful she had lectured herself so thoroughly earlier. As it was, her pulses were tripping over each other.

'Oh, come on, Kate, don't be shy. Your brothers have given you such a great build-up—I was looking forward to a demonstration on the definitive art of tree-climbing.' Kate could very easily learn to hate that amused drawl.

'I have no doubts of my abilities in this direction, Mr Courtney. But there do happen to be other considerations.' Namely these indecently skimpy shorts, she thought, but did not say. She did not have to.

'Well, to be honest, it was those other considerations I was most looking forward to. I have been privileged to look upon a lady's legs before now, you know,' he added softly.

I just bet you have! For one horrified moment Kate thought she had actually said the words out loud, she was so surprised at the vehemence of her thoughts.

'Though I must say, from this angle yours appear to be rather special . . .'

'All right!' Kate closed her eyes in resignation, trying valiantly to ignore the fluttery pleasure his flattery provoked. Gregory Courtney in a playful mood? It really didn't bear thinking about! 'I'm coming!'

She did very well until she was half-way down, living up to all her brothers' boasts, despite the sure knowledge that Gregory Courtney's gaze was riveted on her long limbs. The shiver travelling up her spine told her he was not missing an inch of exposed flesh, roaming over her neatly rounded bottom, and the gap left by the halter top which was riding up to a dangerously indecent level. And of course, she thought half hysterically, I would decide to discard my bra today of all days!

36

Her mother's shriek brought her down a lot faster than she had intended, and she landed in a flurry of tangled limbs, squarely into Gregory Courtney's waiting arms! Waves of mortification spread over her as he began to shake with silent laughter.

'I suppose it was too much to hope that you'd turn your back, Mr Courtney!' she muttered as haughtily as possible in such unedifying circumstances.

'And miss this gift from the gods, Miss McNaught?' he drawled, his voice a deep velvet brown. 'And don't you think we've passed the formality of surnames, Kate?'

'I don't think . . .'

'The name is Greg. Try it—it's quite easy.' Her mouth refused to form the word as she met his compelling gaze. The steely grey eyes pierced through her and she was far too conscious of his hand splayed across the bare skin of her back, and the fingers of his right hand moving seductively around the sensitive skin at the back of her knee. 'Say it, Kate!'

'G-Greg,' she murmured weakly.

He allowed her to stand on her own two feet then, though it was a moot point whether or not she would have been able to stand without his supporting hand at her waist. She was all too conscious of her dishevelled appearance, from her tumbling waves of hair to the skimpy clothes, and her face so shiningly free of make-up. She was not a vain person by any means, but to appear like this to the man one had only just been weaving romantic fantasies about was, to say the least—awful!

But her humiliation was not quite yet complete.

'Really, Katherine! I thought you possessed more sense than to go climbing trees at your age! You're as bad as the boys! Have you thought what an example you're setting them? You know very well I've forbidden them to climb that tree. Whatever will Mr Courtney think of us?'

Kate closed her eyes in despair. 'If you don't mind,' she said haughtily, casting a baleful glance at her two unbelievably innocent-looking brothers, one of whom was gleefully clutching his football, 'I'm going to find a hole to crawl into!'

She made to go into the house, her chin high, although she could feel the back of her neck burning at the thought of the sight she was now presenting to that mocking devil!

'Oh no, you don't, young lady!' Kate groaned. Only her mother could reduce her from a geriatric to a schoolgirl without drawing breath! 'You will go and entertain Mr Courtney, while I see to some cold drinks. Boys, go and fetch your father from the allotments!' The boys ran. One look at Kate's expressionless face was enough to advise them to stay out of sight for some time to come. Unlike Toby Marchant, they had seen that look before!

'This way, Mr . . . Greg,' she said stiffly, after his checking glance. She restrained the urge to smooth down her hair as she dredged her mind for small talk and came up empty. Fortunately, Greg started the conversation.

'I'm sorry to interrupt your—umm—activities, but I have to go to Scotland tomorrow. I'll be away for three or four days, so there are a few things we have to discuss.'

'Yes, of course.' This was better. Kate felt safe talking of business matters. She could pretend they were in the office. He was dressed formally in a dark business suit, not in black suede trousers and claret silk shirt, unbuttoned low enough to allow her a glimpse of hair-roughened chest. And she was not really sitting here in a lime green halter top which clung lovingly to her clearly outlined curves, and a pair of shorts which were to be consigned to the dustbin as soon as she could get rid of . . .

'Kate?'

'Oh, I'm sorry. Did you say something?' She risked a glance through the veil of her lashes, but his mask was back in place. The eyebrows were fairly high, though!

'I was asking about these sketches,' Greg repeated patiently, gesturing to the wall above the fireplace. 'I noticed yesterday that one seemed to be missing.'

Kate looked up at the four sketches fondly. Her parents and brothers.

'Yes, there isn't one of me.'

'Why not?'

'Because I drew them.'

Greg stared at her in surprise. 'I wonder what other talents you're hiding. These are good. They have some indefinable quality . . .'

Kate kept her eyes on the sketches. Greg was right, most people remarked on the pencil drawings. She had managed to capture the chief characteristics of each of her family—her father's gruff belligerence, tempered by a heart as soft as melted butter, her mother gently scolding with that irrepressible smile. And her brothers—mischief incorporated!

'It's love,' she stated without expression, a little embarrassed at explaining. 'I can only do portraits of people I love. The others I've tried simply don't work out. It's the eyes, I think.'

He stared at her intently for a moment. 'So you're a romantic,' he said flatly, as if he was disappointed in her.

She bristled a little but retorted mildly, 'What's romantic about loving your family? Actually, I'm probably the most practical of the bunch, but I do firmly believe that love is the only sound basis for any relationship.'

'So you wouldn't marry for money?'

'Never,' she shuddered. 'I can't imagine anything more sterile. Lack of money has never altered my parents' love for each other—sometimes love was all they had to hold them together. There's no security in a relationship otherwise.'

His head tilted to one side. 'I can see that temper of yours beginning to make an appearance. I wonder why I never noticed it before.'

'Because only things which touch me personally can affect me enough,' she could have said, but he was looking at her in such a devastating way, she decided to play safe and change the subject.

'You said we had things to—er—discuss, Mr—er—Greg.'

Fortunately he allowed her to get away with it. 'Yes, I've brought some proposals for your father and Walsh to look at. We can finalise things when I come back from Scotland then.'

Kate was not surprised at the speed with which he had things organised. Once Greg made up his mind, he acted immediately. She thought happily that it was quite possible her father would be in business before another week had passed.

'I thought we might have dinner together. You haven't eaten yet?'

Caught unawares, she very nearly gaped at him. Was he really asking her for a date?

'No, but . . .'

'You have other plans, perhaps?' His mouth hardened to a thin line.

'Well, not exactly . . .'

'Washing your hair?' he persisted. Kate had a feeling he was forcing the teasing smile on to his lips. But she could not help but smile back.

'No, I washed it this morning. That's why it's so . . .' she gestured graphically.

'I like it,' he murmured, allowing his glance to linger on the unrestrained waves.

'No—it's just that Terry mentioned something about taking me for a drink, but he won't mind if I put him off.' It had only been a tentative arrangement. She knew Terry well enough to realise that if another girl crossed his path during the day—preferably blonde, bosomy, with an IQ to match her bra size!—he too would have called off the outing.

'Put him off what?' Terry demanded from the doorway. 'You wouldn't be trying to wangle your way out of our date, would you, princess? I've been looking forward to this for weeks!'

Kate laughed at his expression of wounded pride. 'Liar!' she scolded. 'You've just been too busy to find anyone with the right qualifications.' Her eyes sparkled as she turned confidingly to Greg. 'Namely a staple through the navel!' Terry's deplorable taste in women was a long-standing joke between them. Neither of them caught the speculative look Greg shot them before his features closed up once more.

'I'm afraid I'm going to pull rank on you, Walsh.' The charming smile was turned on full force. Kate had never before been the focus of that charm, and the warm feeling in the pit of her stomach warned her that she had underestimated its power.

'Ah well,' Terry sighed dramatically, turning to leave, 'I suppose I'll have to make do with the gorgeous blonde I met at lunch-time!' He winked at Kate. 'Don't wait up for me, will you?' And he left, whistling. Kate shook her head fondly. The man was incorrigible!

'Walsh is staying here?'

'Yes,' she answered, a little taken aback at the returning harshness in Greg's voice. 'Just until he finds himself a place.' The fond smile returned to light her features. 'Between you and me, I think he's dragging his feet a little. Mom's cooking is second to none!'

'I see.'

'Well,' she smiled nervously to break the uneasy silence which had fallen, 'I'd better go and change.'

'Don't go to any trouble. We'll be eating at my apartment.' His cool statement had the effect of a lead weight dropping from a great height, as Kate measured all the implications. Greg's lips twisted as he read her expression.

'Don't look so apprehensive, my dear Miss McNaught. I retain a very vivid memory of Toby Marchant's bruised jaw!' Kate relaxed in relief as she was meant to, though she could not help the faint colour spreading over her face at the reminder of that disastrous day——although perhaps it had not been as disastrous as it had first appeared. Hadn't that day been the start of this—Kate found she did not have the words to explain the changing relationship between her and Greg. She only knew she felt poised on the verge of a great adventure.

He came towards her, towering over her to trail warm fingers over her smooth, hot cheek, his thumb dropping to trace the outline of her lips. Her mouth went dry in anticipation of his kiss, but a sound from the kitchen alerted them to imminent interruption and she jumped back, startled.

'I—um—I'll go and change.'

'Oh, Kate,' he called her back softly as she turned to leave the room.

'Yes?' she breathed.

'Leave your hair loose.'

'I—yes.'

Kate gave herself half an hour to get ready, limiting her promised soak in the bath to a scant five minutes. Her make-up took little time—a dab of eye-shadow and a touch of mascara. Her creamy complexion needed no enhancement at all. She had long ago stopped fretting about the freckles dotted over her skin. And she certainly was in no need of blusher. Nature seemed to have taken on that task whenever she was within ten feet of a certain individual!

She did stop for one moment to try frantically to remember all the reasons she had decided to keep her distance from Greg, but all that came to mind was her intention to accept the very next date she was offered. She applied a little lip-gloss, then turned to inspect her wardrobe, which was pitifully slender regarding evening wear. She eventually chose her favourite dress—as she had known she would all along.

She had bought the dress from her very first pay cheque from Courtney's. The sleeveless velour was perfect for the evening. From a rounded neckline the dress clung lovingly to breast and hip, and the skirt flowed to just below the knee in various muted shades of sea green. An obvious choice for a redhead, she knew, but no one could deny the dress was made for her.

Sounds of mirth reached her as she descended the stairs, her green eyes glowing like a cat's. She hugged the sounds to herself, feeling more grateful to Greg than she could possibly say for restoring the cosy harmony which spelt home to her.

'. . . and she used to sit on my knee waving to all the passers by, every inch the Queen of England! That's why we dubbed her "princess". Hey, Callum, do you remember that time we had the vintage cars on the trailer . . .?'

Kate closed her eyes in fond despair as she entered the lounge in time to stop Terry's reminiscent ramblings.

'I think we'd better leave before the family photographs are put on display,' she cut in drily. Her quick glance took in the tableau of Terry with a glass raised to his smiling lips, Greg's obvious difficulty in controlling his mirth, her mother more animated than she had been for months, and her father—looking younger by the minute. He shot Kate a mischievous glance that could have been stolen from either of her brothers, and tapped Greg on the shoulder.

'You must remind me to show you the one of Kate in her grandmother's garden . . .'

'Dad,' Kate wailed, her voice agonised. 'I swear if you ever dare show that photo to anyone . . .!'

'Don't worry, Katherine,' her mother laughed, 'I have it hidden away safely.'

'I think we'd better leave.' Greg eyed Kate sympathetically, and Kate agreed fervently. The sooner they left, the better. She knew her family too well in this mood. Heaven only knew what skeletons had already been dragged out of the family closet!

'Greg,' her father started gruffly as they rose to leave, 'I can't tell you how much we appreciate this chance. We won't let you down, I promise!'

'I have no doubts on that score, Callum,' Greg asserted as they shook hands. 'Any man who can raise a daughter like Kate . . .'

'Oh, please, don't mind me!' Kate's colour rose in indignation, causing Greg to stare fixedly at her. 'I just love been spoken of as the family pet poodle!'

'Oh, never a poodle, Kate. They yap. Besides, with that temper of yours . . .'

'Oh, you've come across our Kate's temper, then, have you, lad?' chuckled Callum. Even Kate had to smile at Greg being referred to as 'lad!' Though he did not seem to mind.

'Let's just say I've seen it in action, Callum. I've never had the full force directed at me—yet,' he added with a strange look at the subject of the conversation.

'Then let me advise you . . .'

'I think Greg can take care of himself, Dad,' Kate put in tartly. She looked up at Greg, a wry curve to her generous lips as she asked plaintively, 'Can we please go? I love my family, but . . .!'

'Of course.' Greg turned back to the older man. 'We'll get together when I return from Scotland. Meanwhile, get in touch with Sam Goodis on Monday morning. I'll liaise with him.'

Kate kissed her parents goodnight—very much on her dignity, as much as she was allowed in this family—then spoilt the effect by poking out her tongue at Terry.

'Be good, children!' He gave them his blessing as Kate

swirled past, embarrassed, infuriated and happier than she could remember being for a long time.

Kate's uneasiness returned as they travelled in the lift up to Greg's penthouse apartment. He was far too close for comfort, his tall, lean frame lazing indolently in the corner, hooded eyes missing none of her apprehensions. Once inside the apartment, Kate was more able to relax, having put a little distance between them. Looking around her with interest, she was disappointed to find the apartment as cold and impersonal as she had once thought Greg to be.

It was luxurious enough by any standards, certainly it had cost a small fortune to decorate and furnish the place. But it was a mere shell, totally lacking in the character Kate looked for in a home. There were no personal touches, nothing to indicate that Greg had ever lived there. Kate found she much preferred the shabbier but welcoming home her family occupied.

'You don't like it here, do you?' Her host once more divined her thoughts.

Kate prevaricated, 'It's not for me to like or dislike, is it?'

'No matter,' he shrugged. 'What can I get you to drink? Martini?'

'Gin and tonic,' she corrected, feeling in need of a stronger drink. His brows rose.

'I didn't realise you were a hardened drinker, Kate.'

'Oh, I manage to keep it under control at work,' she quipped lightly, finding him dangerously attractive in this teasing mood. She nibbled nervously at her bottom lip. 'I know you don't want my thanks for what you've done, Greg . . .'

'Then don't give them!' he told her bluntly, his tone reverting to the harsher sound she was more accustomed to.

'But . . .'

He sighed in exasperation, handing her a glass. 'Sit down.' he ordered. 'Kate, would it make you feel better if I told you I had a selfish motive for what I did?'

'I don't understand.' She could also see he did not want to explain further. He was staring broodingly into his drink, the teasing manner he had adopted at her home having vanished completely.

'Your father reminds me of someone I once knew, a man who had only his pride to live on. I had to stand and watch as that pride was chipped away, piece by piece, until he was left with nothing.' He took a long swallow of his drink. 'I wouldn't like to repeat the process with your father as the victim. He's a good man, Kate.'

'Oh, Greg!' Kate was very moved by his words. Obviously this was a way for him to come to terms with his previous impotence to help. She wondered briefly about the man who could affect Greg strongly enough for him to take her father's predicament so much to heart. His own father, perhaps? Unfortunately, the tense set of his jaw, the downward-slanting brows, indicated his unwillingness to expand, and Kate was too sensitive to pry further.

But what a complex man he was becoming! Not at all the cold, remote figure she had always thought. There was so much seething below the surface, so much she had yet to discover, if he would allow it.

He shrugged off his jacket now, making Kate irritably aware of the hard muscles rippling under the claret silk shirt.

'There's a very obliging restaurant just around the corner from here,' he said lightly, handing her a menu card.

'Mmm, I'm impressed.' She pulled a face at him. 'I take it you prefer not to cook yourself?'

'I can if I put my mind to it. But this saves on the washing up!'

As good a reason as any, if one could afford it, Kate agreed silently.

She ordered melon and grilled sole—hardly an inspired choice, but her stomach was behaving very strangely, causing her appetite to all but disappear. Greg ordered steak.

'That was delicious!' she declared an hour later, helping him to dispose of the foil wrappers in his ultra-modern kitchen. She refused liqueurs, preferring to mop up a little of the wine she had drunk with the coffee Greg was making.

The relaxed atmosphere between them over dinner began to dissipate the moment Greg ushered her back into the huge lounge. A little flustered, Kate sank back into the comfort of a large leather armchair, drawing her feet up under her. He chose to sit directly opposite her.

'What was it you wanted to discuss, Greg? The pay talks?' she asked softly as the silence began to grate on her nerves.

'No—Sam will be handling those until I return,' he answered quietly, his gaze intent on her. 'I didn't bring you here to discuss business, Kate.'

'Then . . .' She swallowed the nervous lump lodged in her throat, not at all sure she wanted an answer to the question she was about to put.

'I'm sure if you search the dark recesses of your mind you could come up with something approaching the truth.'

Kate went very still. Even without his confirming words, the blatant message flashing in the taunting brilliance of his hooded eyes needed no further explanation. Whatever she had expected this evening to bring—and if she were brutally honest with herself, she had hoped for more than business to be on the agenda—it had certainly not been this full-blown assault. Greg sat back at his ease, reading the varying emotions chasing across her features with an accuracy that would have embarrassed her had she known.

'Don't worry, Kate!' His harsh voice dropped into the fraught silence. 'I'm not demanding payment for helping your father.'

'Did you really think . . .?' Kate broke off, annoyed at the croak that issued from her throat.

'Well, a man can but hope.' The laconic lift of his eyebrow hardly indicated defeat, but it did allow her to breathe a little easier, knowing he was not entirely serious. 'I suppose I should apologise, but I'm not going to. That blush of yours is so delightful, it's rather difficult to resist the temptation to tease it into full bloom.'

'You're not exactly teasing, though, are you?' Quite why she was so certain, Kate could not say. Two years of watching him at work, perhaps? But she did silently berate herself for being so blunt without considering the deeper implications. She felt such a strong reluctance to be left in the dark about his plans for her. The need to know exactly where she stood with this remote, infinitely disturbing man was too strong to resist.

'If by that do I mean I expect you to—bestow your favours, shall we say, in exchange for your father's loan . . .' His voice had reached that dangerously soft, calm level she knew spelt trouble.

'No, that's not what I meant, and you know it!' Kate's indignation was at too high a point to be easily dismissed. 'You're perfectly well aware that I would never consider such an arrangement.'

'Yes, I suppose I was,' Greg murmured absently, almost to himself. Kate's growing irritation was temporarily soothed by his grudging admission, but all her senses went back on full alert at his next words. 'Just what would it take to get you into my bed, Kate?'

The blush Greg found so delightful took a moment to make its inevitable appearance. Her face drained of colour before becoming suffused once more in a rosy hue. She dumped her coffee-cup with a lamentable lack of ceremony on the small table before her and surged to her feet, not quite knowing what she intended to do, but certain she could no longer remain immobile.

'There are more normal ways to go about this, you know,' she ventured, striving for as light a tone as possible to counterbalance the growing tension swirling about them. She was not so innocent that she had never been propositioned before, but never quite so boldly. And never with such an arrogant assumption that she would agree to it!

'Ah, you want to be wined and dined, do you, Kate? Have me send flowers and all the rest of that ridiculous rigmarole?' His manner indicated that such manoeuvres were a total waste of time and effort. Obviously his blunt business methods came into play on more intimate occasions, Kate thought, with wry amusement overshadowing the more disturbing undercurrents for the moment.

'Oh, those old seduction techniques have their uses, believe me, Greg,' she murmured a little shakily. 'At least they provide a warning of intent!'

His head inclined in acknowledgement of her point, a small smile playing around his lips as he registered her agitation.

'But I don't want to seduce you, Kate. I want you to come to me with your eyes wide open. I could have put you on notice when you first came to work for me, but we would have reached this point sooner or later.'

'You mean you've . . .?' The words refused to even form. 'That long?'

His compelling gaze refused to allow her to look away for even a moment. Again, what she saw in his eyes was confirmed by his words.

'I've wanted you since the first moment I set eyes on you!'

'Then why . . .?'

'Why wait so long before making a move?' She nodded slowly, no longer trusting her vocal cords.

He held her eyes by sheer force of personality, his own glittering, confident, anticipatory, hers open, bewildered—and very vulnerable.

'You weren't ready, Kate,' he averred softly, coming slowly to his feet with such intent of purpose she forgot to breathe, her whole being poised for his touch. It came slowly, insidiously, gentle fingers threading through the tumbling waves of red hair at her nape. 'You were so very young, Kate. So very shy. So very damned innocent. You would have turned in your resignation and run as far and as fast as you were able.'

He was right. It was possible she still would—if she could only move!

'And you became the perfect secretary—cool, efficient, impersonal. I can see now that you had problems at home which distracted you. But when I discovered you punching Marchant on the jaw . . .'

'You decided the time was right?'

'No,' he denied softly, his eyes darkening. 'I very simply found my patience had run out!'

'And what makes you think I'm ready now?' Talking was difficult over the nervous lump in her throat. Her voice emerged as little more than a whisper, as every cell in her body screamed awareness of his dangerous proximity, the woodsy flavour of his aftershave teasing her nostrils.

'I doubt if you are. Sometimes . . .' His hand smoothed down the line of her throat, thumbs absently tracing her quickening pulses, 'sometimes I doubt you'll ever be ready for me, Kate.'

'I don't understand!'

'Is understanding so important, Kate? Try feeling.' Slowly, inexorably, he was exerting the tiniest pressure to tilt her chin to his lowering head, until their lips were a mere breath away. 'Give me your mouth, Kate!'

'I——Oh!' Her words were smothered by his lips. Taking full advantage of her bemused vulnerability, Greg relinquished all hold on his immense self-control, and plundered the treasure beneath his lips and hands, losing himself in the beckoning warmth of her softness. Sensations she had never before experienced cascaded throughout her entire body as his lips ravaged the soft inner flesh of her mouth, his tongue meeting hers in a duel of possession, taking away all thought, leaving only sensory intoxication.

Her fingers fluttered helplessly for long moments before instinctively finding their rightful place behind his head to cleave him to her, to become lost in the rich darkness of his hair.

There was a momentary loss of balance, of floating through the air, then she was sinking into the sumptuous thickness of the cream carpet, the warm strands soothing against her naked back. Then suddenly, shockingly, his hand was at her breast, moulding the soft contour with exquisite hunger until her helpless whimper gave him pause, and his hands and mouth gentled, soothing her, though still arousing and still insistent upon a response Kate had no way of denying.

Then he moved on to her. Brought into full electrifying awareness of his throbbing need, Kate began to shake—violently, from fear, desire, she knew not which. She only knew, with fatalistic certainty, that he was right. She was not ready, never would be ready, for this all-consuming passion he evoked.

Taken by surprise, Greg drew back sharply, and swore violently as her panic-filled face came into focus. Even in her befuddled state, Kate could see the immense effort it cost him to draw back in the taut lines of his body, as he sucked in breaths to control his desire.

His shirt was unbuttoned, half hanging out of his trousers,

and Kate groaned aloud as the memory hit her of running her hands over that muscled chest, her fingertips tangling in the crisp dark hairs.

Dragging her eyes from his tense immobile figure, she jumped up, intent on putting as much distance as possible between them, and ran for the bathroom. Shakily, half afraid of what she would see, she peered into the mirror, wincing at the sight reflected back.

Her hair was in total disarray, her make-up non-existent, her mouth slightly swollen from Greg's passionate onslaught. But her eyes told the full story, still holding all the erotic pleasure he had evoked from a body she had actually once considered frigid!

Nothing in Kate's life had prepared her for the tumultuous sensations Greg had forced from her. She, who had always prided herself on her level-headedness, unable to understand the friends who had confided the ease with which they had been carried away on a storm of feeling.

But oh, how well she understood now! Had he been a man of lesser integrity, he could have taken her with humiliating ease, ignoring her fears. She could only feel tremendous gratitude that he had not forced the issue. It would be difficult enough to face him as it was.

Preparing herself for the confrontation, she splashed cold water on her overheated face and tried desperately to bring some sort of order to what was supposed to be her crowning glory.

Greg was pacing the floor like a caged tiger when Kate had finally summoned up the courage to face him. His look of concern warmed her, though, prompting her to voice her thanks.

'For what?' Greg's husky voice was incredulous, though it still retained a measure of the memory of holding her trembling body in his arms. 'Frightening you half to death?' His mouth twisted in self-disgust, and Kate's soft heart contracted painfully.

'No, Greg, I'm thanking you for stopping when you did. You must know . . .' She hung her head, unable to complete her confession. Greg shook his head slowly in disbelief at her soft gratitude.

'I never meant to let things get out of hand like that, Kate . . .' He held up a hand to stay her interruption. 'No, hear me out.' The brows were at last beginning their ascent. 'It may be your one and only opportunity to ever hear me apologise, so you'd better make the most of it.' He indicated that she should be seated but, try as she might, she could not completely relax. So she sat opposite him, not trusting herself to be any closer to him.

The wry glance he shot her told her he had received the message. Lazing back in his chair, he made a quick, thorough survey of her.

She had not recovered yet, by any means, he thought, cursing himself for losing control at such a critical time, and wondering for the thousandth time just what this girl-woman possessed that affected him so powerfully. Her hands were still trembling, he noted with satisfaction. And that lower lip was quivering so very slightly, causing his body to tauten once more with remembered passion of the sweetness of those lips.

No, there was no time for patient wooing, even if such games appealed to him. Now that he had been allowed a glimpse of the smouldering hunger she could ignite, he wanted all of it. Soon. And on his own terms.

'I'm afraid I forgot to take into account just how very much I want you, Kate. Once you gave me your mouth I was lost.' His voice was soft and deep, deceptively sincere, a warm light entering those habitually cold eyes as they ranged over her, reading every nuance of her still, straight figure, her luminous bewildered eyes, the unnatural pallor of her soft skin. 'Your—um—response came as something of a surprise.'

Her head snapped up, colour surging back into her face with indignation—just as he had intended.

'Is that the best you can do?' she spluttered, forgetting for the moment that he spoke no less than the truth. Surprise was a mild word to use. Greg merely shrugged, his expression deadpan.

'I've had so very little practice at apologising.'

Kate had to laugh despite the fraught state of her nervous

system. Why had she never noticed that dry, understated humour before?

'Oh, Greg!' she moaned. 'This isn't a laughing matter, you know. I feel dreadful!'

'Oh, Kate!' he mimicked her. 'Is it so unbelievable that I might want you?' Pinned by that compelling gaze, Kate could only nod, then she tried to lighten the atmosphere again.

'Would it be very crass of me to say, "But this is so sudden, Mr Courtney"?'

'We've known each other for over two years, Kate!' he rasped impatiently, refusing to respond to her lighter tone, and allowing the electric tension to return.

'Yes. But not like this!' She took a deep, wavering breath to still her agitation.

'What is it you're afraid of, Kate?'

'I'm not sure. I am serious about this being sudden, Greg, even if it does sound clichéd. The way you make me feel, it——Oh, glory!' She exhaled in exasperation, too wound up to even think straight, let alone verbalise her fears. She turned eventually to face him, grateful that he had given her time to compose herself. Despite her emotional vulnerability, she was determined not to let him ride roughshod over her raw feelings. If, as she suspected, he conducted his private life on the same basis as his business life, she could expect him to go for the jugular at any moment.

'What exactly do you want from me, Greg? A one-night stand? A casual fling? A deep and meaningful relationship? What?'

Greg watched her attempt at dignity with brooding intensity, a glimmer of anger showing in his eyes, as if that was the last question he wanted to answer.

'I haven't quite worked that out for myself, yet, but . . . Hell, Kate, don't look at me like that!'

Kate did not know what he was talking about. 'I don't . . .'

'There's one thing I'm sure about, Kate. I don't want you to confuse this—desire for anything more than it is.'

Kate's face burned. Just what had he seen written on her unguarded features? She was not used to hiding her feelings. She drew herself up.

'It almost sounds as if you're warning me against you.'

'Only against you imagining yourself in love with me, Kate.' Her head lifted proudly in the face of his hard words.

'Surely that could only be to your benefit!'

He shook his head firmly. 'Oh, no, Kate. I've seen what so-called love can do to people like you. I don't want to put you through the same hell my f . . .' He broke off, raking his fingers through his dark hair. 'Quite surprisingly, I've discovered I have a few scruples where you're concerned, Kate. I won't lie to you. I want you very badly, but I'm simply not capable of any more than that. It wouldn't be a brief fling,' his eyes dropped the length of her body, 'and neither would it be casual. Personally I don't give a damn what name you put to it.'

Kate could only applaud his frankness, while flinching inwardly at the sterile sort of relationship he proposed. She supposed she should feel flattered that he liked her enough to be honest. She had a feeling that that was not quite written into the script for this evening. For the very first time in her life she wished she had some experience to fall back on.

She had played at love quite light-heartedly before her duties at Courtney's had become so demanding that she had needed all her spare time to recoup her energies for the next set of contractual negotiations, making her such lousy company for anyone unfortunate enough to date her at that time she had more often than not declined invitations out.

Not one of her dates had ever prepared her for the likes of Gregory Courtney. None had elicited more than a lukewarm response at best. And never had she regretted turning down their more insistent demands, assuming she was simply not the stuff of which great passions were made.

Greg had shattered that myth once and for all, in the space of one short evening, giving her sight of a side of her nature she had never known existed. She could see now, with hindsight, that it was not her own fastidious nature which had caused her to refuse all strong advances, but a simple lack of temptation. Oh, she had been curious enough about the subject which dominated most of her friends' conversations since schooldays, but never enough to experiment for the sake of it.

But she was tempted now—oh, so tempted to nod her head, knowing that was all it would take for Greg to gather her back into his arms to again work that potent magic on her still roused senses.

But, even in her sexual naïveté, she knew this would be no simple sharing of bodies. Even as he gave her pleasure, he would take it back one hundredfold, using her passion against her, rather than to fulfil them both. He would totally dominate any relationship he embarked upon, and when he was finished with her he would have no compunction about leaving her to face a life without him. Kate shuddered at the picture. She must be mad to even think of such a course of action—to give herself to him with no thoughts of all the tomorrows he refused to even consider.

'No!' The word left her lips without volition. But she meant it! 'Greg, I'm not cut out for this kind of relationship. You must see that!'

'What's stopping you? Your parents?' he bit out, a sarcastic edge creeping into his voice. 'Don't you think you're old enough to cut the apron strings, Kate?'

'Yes. But I would still hesitate to hurt them in such a way. Besides, that's only part of it.' She held his gaze, silently entreating his understanding of her reservations. What else could she say? 'I'm frightened I might fall in love with you—when you refuse to consider the word even relevant?' If he had registered her plea he gave no sign of it. His expression was fixed along grim, implacable lines.

'There's our working relationship to consider . . .'

'That wouldn't change—unless you wanted to leave. I'd be quite happy to set you up in a flat, Kate . . .'

'You just stop right there!' His head shot up at her vehement attack. 'I'm no man's plaything, Gregory Courtney! And I never will be. If you think you can buy me . . .'

'That isn't what I was suggesting at all!' Kate did not hear him, intent as she was on keeping hold of her wayward temper. 'Kate, if you're worried whether or not I'll still respect you in the morning . . .' He bit off an explicit epithet as he caught the glimmer of tears on her thick lashes, and went to kneel before her, grasping her chin to force her to look directly at him, frustratingly aware that she was at the end of her emotional tether.

'Listen to me, Kate! I happen to have a great respect for you. That's the reason I refuse to entice you into my bed with lies and empty promises. I enjoy your company. You're a very stimulating person to be around. I also happen to like you, which is a damn sight more than I feel for most people. But I can't change who or what I am. I can't promise you happy-ever-after in an ivy-covered country cottage with the expected two point five children, however much you deserve it.

'Anything else that is in my power to give you, I will. Anything short of love and marriage and all that hogwash. I can promise that for as long as our relationship lasts I'll be faithful to you. I'm no more keen on casual sex than you are.' His voice lowered to a more intimate intensity. 'And I can certainly promise you that we'd be dynamite together, Kate. You felt that as well as I.' He rose, bringing her to her feet, but retaining his hold on her shoulder. 'I'm taking you home now. I should be back from Scotland on Wednesday—Thursday at the latest. We'll talk then.'

'Greg, there's really no point . . .'

'We'll talk when I get back, Kate.'

And, as usual, he had the last word.

CHAPTER FOUR

THE NEXT few days proved rather anticlimatic. Kate had always vaguely missed Greg's presence on the other occasions he had been called away. Impersonal as he was, he brought a spirit of dynamism into the office, a sense of anticipation, of excitement even. Now she was counting the hours until his return, anxious to bring this period of insanity to a close.

For that, surely, was all it could be? Some sort of aberration? A very compelling one, to be sure, but madness, none the less. That was what the logical part of her brain told her. Her logic slipped, however, when she thought back over the two years she had known Greg.

For some reason, their first meeting was indelibly printed upon her mind. Even now she could feel the laughter freezing in her throat as she had looked up one day to the sight of those steely grey eyes fixed upon her. He had absorbed her at a single glance. Her co-workers, whose laughter she had been sharing, had all fallen silent when he asked for her by name.

'I've wanted you since the first moment I set eyes on you!'

Yes, Kate could believe it now. Could see the hidden sexual assessment in the glance she had previously been too innocent, too overwhelmed, to decipher.

She had badly needed the job he offered. Her father had already been out of work for twelve months and their savings had dwindled to a dangerously low level. And, though Greg had been very patient in those first weeks, Kate had felt it necessary to prove herself indispensable. Which she had, if his mood on her returns from vacations were anything to go by! Her family's need for the commensurate increase in her salary had allowed nothing to interfere with her concentration on the job in hand.

They worked well together. Between them, they had developed a mental shorthand, Kate more often than not knowing his decisions the moment he made them. The flicker of an eyelash, the arching of a brow, the way he held himself—she became attuned to his body language.

So why had she failed to pick up the sexual signals before now? Or had she subconsciously known they would be too dangerous to interpret, and ignored them as she had the occasional frisson of excitement she had experienced when she looked at him? And those dissecting surveys of his, had she deliberately decided to view them as punishment rather than the test she now knew them to be?

So many little things were now falling into place that she felt she must have been wearing blinkers for the past two years.

'You weren't ready then, Kate,' he had said. And so he proceeded to put her to the test—just occasionally—until the first moment her composure slipped. And then he had pounced so swiftly she had not been allowed time to think.

'This breathing space is exactly what you need,' she told herself a thousand times. Why then the impatience to see him—to tell him of her decision?

Unfortunately, Kate was only too well aware of the answer. She was still tempted.

The pictures still flashed through her mind's eye, in vivid Technicolor, of how she had instinctively arched into him the moment he touched her, of the instantaneous, intolerable excitement which left her aching when he drew back. She even began to wish that he had ignored her fears, so that she would have a true concept of what she was turning down.

She would have thought long and hard about entering a physical relationship with anyone. That was her nature. She liked—needed—to think things through, to weigh up the pros and cons. Which was why she supposed she should have felt grateful for Greg's devastating honesty. It should have made her decision so much easier. It didn't. And that frightened her.

In the idle imaginings most girls indulged in from time to time about their ideal man, Kate had always thought more along the lines of kinship of spirit than sexual compatibility. She had blithely assumed that the physical expression of love would grow from the seeds of friendship, shared interests, mutual respect and affection—as in her parents' marriage. The security of knowing that one's happiness was in safe keeping, anchored to such sturdy foundations. An insurance policy really. The McNaughts had always been great believers in insurance.

And, as appallingly easy as it had become to see Greg as her lover, she could in no way imagine him as her friend. Her protector—yes. He had said he was being honest to protect her from the misery that falling in love with him could bring her. But her friend, equal partners in every way—never.

It seemed so ironic that all her previous friendships with men had been just that—friendship, sex being totally absent from her feelings towards them. But, with Greg, sex would be the only ingredient in an otherwise sterile relationship. If she could only find a combination of the two, she would not hesitate for a moment. Was she destined to go on searching for something that did not exist?

Kate did not know the answer. She was very aware that, in rejecting Greg, she might well be losing her one and only opportunity to fully explore the dormant sensuality he had only just begun to disturb. They were physically compatible to a degree she found earth-shattering. But sex for its own sake was simply not enough for Kate.

Had she been in love with Greg, she honestly believed she would have followed him anywhere, with or without a ring to bind them. The question of marriage would not have affected her answer to any great extent. Nor would her parents' disapproval, contrary to Greg's views on the subject. Although she would have been reluctant to hurt them by indulging in a sexual relationship outside marriage, she was independent—and stubborn—enough to follow her own convictions, rather than her parents' conventions. She was also certain that they would respect any such decision she made enough to accept it. But she did need a commitment of sorts. A commitment of caring—on both sides.

And, whatever it was she felt for Greg, she was positive it could not be love. There was a certain physical infatuation—it would be useless to deny it. He was an extremely attractive man, outwardly.

But mere looks had never weighed much with Kate. Being

by nature a warm, giving person, she found his remoteness vaguely off-putting. Even worse was his unwillingness to compromise. Had she thought there was a chance for love to grow between them, she might very well have decided to take the plunge, or at least requested the time for a relationship to develop naturally, before committing herself physically. But she knew there would never be any more between them than Greg had already promised. A man of his word, was Greg. And he had had the benefit of two years to contemplate the sort of relationship he wanted, not a paltry few days.

She did wish she knew what had happened in his past to turn him into such a remote figure. She was so very ignorant of his family background. The little she had gleaned in the past week made her wonder about his childhood. When he had told her that story about the man who reminded him of Callum, she had felt sure he was talking about his own father—a subject which was obviously distressing for him to discuss.

A miserable childhood would certainly account for his cynicism towards marriage. Or was it perhaps rooted in his later relationships with women? Did every woman he contemplated taking to his bed receive the warning? Kate thought not.

She had the uneasy impression she was a total departure from his usual choice of women, but that was based solely on conjecture. The office grapevine was notorious as a rumour mill, but there had never been so much as a whisper of gossip concerning Greg's affairs. There had, of course, been the usual speculation about how long it would take Kate to fall for her boss, her own dislike of inter-office relationships, and her weekly lunches with Greg, having fuelled the flames of conjecture for a while. But those titbits of gossip had soon died down for simple lack of credible evidence. Until recently, Greg's manner towards her had never failed to be most correct.

She was very tempted to search out Sam Goodis to answer some of those niggling questions about Greg's background; despite the disparity in their ages, the two were very easy in each other's company. But Kate could not overcome her own respect for Greg's privacy. It would be one thing for him to offer the information himself, but quite another for her to go seeking it. Besides, she liked Sam and would be very loath to put him in such an untenable position.

No, there were simply too many cons and too few pros to provide balance. Every instinct of self-preservation screamed for her to keep a safe distance between them.

Their working relationship would be bound to suffer; Kate could not compartmentalise her life in the same way she suspected Greg did. And she certainly could not afford to leave her job.

Her self-respect would not allow her to be a 'kept woman', as Greg had offered. The only men she would ever allow to pay her bills were her father, and whoever one day became her husband. Even then she would hope for some kind of financial independence.

So even the basic logistics of an affair were against them. Kate would not be in a position to leave home at least until Callum and Terry's business got off the ground. And as for explaining to her mother where she was spending her nights——! Besides, she did not want to leave home. She enjoyed the give and take of family life, the companionship, the support of people she loved—and who loved her—temper, warts and all!

Greg would turn her life upside down and inside out. And for what? Excitement? A sexual education? They surely could not outweigh the arguments against. Could they?

Having made up her mind, it was unsettling to say the least to have to wait three or four days before talking to Greg again. She had difficulty concentrating on the simplest of tasks because her mind kept insisting on re-enacting the stomach-churning exhilaration of their last evening together.

It did not help matters that Greg was the main topic of conversation in the McNaught household over the next few days. Kate had to literally bite her tongue to smother the desire to blurt out that Greg was no saint, that he had probably only offered to help as a softening-up gesture designed to lead her to his bed. But she knew that had no basis in fact. Greg could very easily have used her gratitude against her, could have made her feel extremely guilty about turning him down after all he had done for her family. But there had been no hint of such coercion. On the contrary, he had made a point of dismissing her thanks out of hand.

She could have put that down to sensitivity, but with her instinctive knowledge of his business practices she suspected that it merely occupied a separate compartment in his mind. The loan to Callum was filed under business. Kate's file-heading was a different matter altogether! Anyway, she could not bring herself to do anything to burst Callum's bubble of pride. How could she ever justify deflating his self-esteem, and with it, her mother's happiness?

And so, all in all, it was with a feeling of relief, tempered with just a hint of trepidation, that she reached the office the following Thursday morning to find Greg already ensconced in conference with Sam Goodis.

There was no opportunity for a private conversation that morning. Greg's return brought with it the usual flurry of work—all of it urgent, of course. For one brief moment, Kate wondered if she had been hallucinating, and that the events of Saturday evening were a mere figment of her imagination, so normal did everything seem. Then, half-way through the morning, after Greg had ushered out the regional sales supervisors, he looked at her properly for the first time that day. It was a brief look, but all-encompassing, taking in the violet shadows under her eyes caused by nights of tossing and turning instead of sleeping. The dove grey suit she wore, while smart in the extreme, had the unfortunate effect of draining her face of much-needed colour.

He, of course, looked as imperturbable as ever, she thought waspishly, resenting his ability to act as if nothing had happened between them. Even his brows gave nothing away today.

'Send your father and Walsh in as soon as they arrive, would you? I have some calls to make in the meantime.' Kate had forgotten that this was the big day. Terry and Callum were coming to sign the contracts drawn up while Greg was away.

'Yes, of course,' she answered automatically. 'Greg . . .'

'Not now, Kate,' he glanced at his watch impatiently. 'We'll talk at lunch. Have something sent up from the canteen.'

'Yessir!' Kate muttered under her breath, and added a mock salute to his back for good measure. She wondered ironically if she had not been hasty in thinking their working relationship would be in danger of changing had her answer been different. What had she expected? Kisses behind the filing cabinet? Hardly! She must have been mad to even consider it!

She was halfway through explaining a complex report on inter-departmental staff changes to her assistant, Susan, when Terry's cheery voice made her jump. She looked him up and down appreciatively.

'Well, well. Terence Walsh in a suit! I never thought I'd see the day!' She grinned at his spectacularly smart appearance, as he obliged her by giving a little twirl. Callum was self-consciously fingering the knot on his tie and Kate automatically moved forward to straighten it for him.

'So—today's the day, eh, lass?'

'Yes indeed, Dad!' she smiled at him. In more ways than one, she added to herself.

'I didn't realise you were so important, princess. This office is a bit of all right, isn't it?' Terry looked around him with interest, especially towards Susan Henshaw, who was doing her best to shrink into invisibility.

'She's engaged!' Kate muttered to Terry, whose eyes had brightened with a light she read all too easily.

'Ah, well,' he perched nonchalantly on the edge of Kate's desk. 'I don't suppose you fancy giving up all this luxury to come and work in our tin shack, do you?' he asked guilelessly, his voice something less than discreet. Kate noticed the knob on Greg's office door begin to turn. 'The pay would be pretty lousy,' he continued seriously, then his eyebrows waggled in Groucho Marx fashion, 'but think of the fringe benefits, sweetheart!'

'You wouldn't be trying to steal my assistant by any chance, would you, Walsh?'

Terry fell immediately silent at the interruption. Kate intercepted a very strange speculative look passing between her friend and her would-be lover. Terry, for once utterly serious, tilted his head to one side, casting a quick glance in Kate's direction.

'No—Greg.' He turned back. 'Kate always likes to make her own decisions.'

Greg's eyes narrowed, the brows lowering ominously. 'I'll bear that in mind. Callum—it's good to see you again! Come in, the contracts are ready.'

Kate did not realise she was holding her breath until the upward slanting of Greg's eyebrows gave her permission to exhale.

'And just what was that all about?' She pulled Terry back as he made to follow the others into the inner sanctum.

'Men's talk,' he replied airily. 'Don't you worry your pretty little head about it, princess!' And he ducked to ward off the playful punch which inevitably followed such patronage. Kate ground her teeth.

And why do I have the feeling that I've just missed something very significant? she thought. Would she ever understand men? Sometimes she felt the male of the species might as well have just descended from outer space for all the sense they made!

'Kate? We need your signature too!' Greg called her attention back to business.

'Coming!'

Kate had never felt less like eating in her life. Normally nothing affected her healthy appetite, but, just lately, the food seemed to stick in her throat.

Callum had left the office a very happy man about half an hour earlier. Kate wished she could have felt more enthusiastic about the celebration her mother was planning for that evening. Unaccountably, she had not realised that Greg would be receiving an invitation—it could prove rather awkward after this particular interview. At least in the office they could both don their professional masks, but Kate did not have the experience to carry out the social niceties with aplomb. She would have to take her cue from Greg.

She rearranged the sandwiches on her plate yet again, before admitting defeat and replacing her plate on the canteen tray.

'Well, Kate,' drawled Greg after polishing off his share of

the sandwiches, 'I can see the word "no" stamped clearly on your forehead. Like to fill me in on the reasons?' He sounded bored, as if her objections were merely academic. Kate felt her temperature rise immediately.

'Damn you, Greg!' she retorted angrily. He had no right to be so composed when she felt as if she were falling apart. 'Will you stop reading my mind?'

'Am I wrong?' he asked with a cynical sneer she longed to wipe off his face.

'No, you're not wrong,' she breathed finally, taking a sip of coffee to fortify herself. 'I'm afraid I'm simply not sophisticated enough for the sort of arrangement you have in mind. Greg, I . . .' She balked at the next words for a moment, but still faced him bravely, her chin lifted proudly. 'I can't deny that I find you attractive, but . . .' She bristled as he snorted derisively, and slammed his cup back on its saucer without a thought for the fragility of the china. 'OK—I want you! Now are you satisfied?'

'Hardly!' His eyes narrowed with hated amusement.

'It's not enough, Greg. Not for me.' Her tight voice finally got through to him. But aside from a thinning of his lips at her obvious misery, his expression remained impassive.

'Why?'

'You know why, Greg. You must have known before you asked me, or you wouldn't have felt the need to warn me about becoming—emotionally involved. I—I admit I was tempted——' She had to stop, her voice was threatening to crack. Greg's proximity was getting to her. She had sat so many times with him like this and totally blocked out the fact that he was an eminently attractive man. Why couldn't she do it now? Deliberately she turned her mind to all the things he was not offering her. All those things which made a relationship worthwhile pursuing even if, ultimately, they failed—love, caring, friendship, putting one's partner's happiness before one's own. He wasn't even offering partnership, for heaven's sake!

There was a strong rebellious streak in Kate McNaught which had never fully been tested. But it came to the fore now, straightening her backbone both physically and mentally.

'I've done a lot of soul-searching over the past few days, Greg. No doubt you think it rather silly in this day and age to have reservations about sharing my body. But you see, that's what it would be for me. Sharing—total sharing. And I'm not talking about worldly goods here,' she added with a touch of belligerence as he was about to interrupt.

'I realise that, Kate,' he said quietly, surprising her with his sincerity.

Her eyes dropped for a moment, her indignation seeping away. 'Good. I can't give my body lightly, Greg, however much I'm tempted.' A slight flush pinkened her cheekbones as she spoke. She was not in the habit of speaking so frankly about such intimate matters. 'I find I need some sort of commitment—not marriage, necessarily, but at the very least, some degree of—caring. You've been honest with me about your feelings, and I do appreciate that, Greg,' she told him earnestly, holding his eyes, though they told her nothing of his feelings. 'But I can't . . .'

'I get the point!'

He rose and walked over to the window. It was a favourite position of his, as if he drew strength from being able to survey part of the empire he had carved for himself.

Kate had deliberately kept her eyes fixed to his throughout her halting explanation, the better to read his reaction, but it was only now, as she was able to watch him unobserved, that she could see he was not as unaffected by her rejection of his proposition as she had previously thought.

His fists were jammed into the trouser pockets of his dark grey suit, his jaw was set tight, a muscle working along the edge.

'As a matter of fact, I had second thoughts myself, while I was away,' he told her.

'You did?' It was a little dog-in-the-mangerish to feel disappointment at his words, but Kate could not prevent a note of pique from colouring her voice. Greg turned to face her, leaning back against the wall, and watched her closely.

'It occurred to me that it might be a little difficult to conduct the sort of affair I had in mind while you're still living with your parents . . .'

'Well, yes. I mean . . . I thought of that too,' she finished lamely, her eyes dropping before the lazy mockery she could see in his face.

'It also occurred to me that Callum would be rather upset if he were to learn that he was, in effect, taking money from his daughter's lover.'

Kate took a much-needed gulp of coffee to moisten her dry mouth. She hadn't thought of that. And of course Greg was right. But did he have to be so—blunt?

'I think,' she said carefully, 'I think he'd rather spend the rest of his life on the dole.'

And their glances met for one long timeless second before Kate dragged her way out of his hypnotic gaze.

'You do see it's impossible, don't you, Greg?'

'That scenario, yes.'

'I don't und . . .'

A slow sensual smile crept over his features as he watched her battle with confusion, but his voice was as dispassionate as ever as he concluded, 'So I've decided the best solution is for us to marry.'

He watched with great interest the variety of emotions which chased across her face in quick succession, reading each and every one with ridiculous ease. Stunned amazement, a slight dawning of something he preferred not to interpret, and then—unexpectedly, the total blankness he had last seen the second before she had punched Toby Marchant on the jaw!

'Marriage!' The initial shock which almost sent Kate tumbling off her chair was swiftly replaced by an ominously calm feeling of—nothing. Very carefully, as if her life depended on it, she placed her cup and saucer in the centre of the canteen tray.

'Tell me, Greg, does this—amazingly generous offer include happy-ever-after in that country cottage with those inevitable two point five children?' she asked sweetly, for once not giving a hoot that his brows were entering the red alert area. 'Or do the same rules still apply?'

'Yes, they still apply,' he answered in an even tone.

'I see!' she hissed. 'So this—marriage, for want of a better word, would exist only on paper and in bed. Is that the idea?'

His lids dropped, lazily veiling his expression, but Kate could sense the anger begin to surround him as if it were actually palpable. She was way past caring about the consequences. She was as icily furious as she had ever been in her life.

'I do believe you're losing your temper, Miss McNaught!' he mocked.

'I do believe you're right, Mr Courtney,' she answered in the same ironical tone, unconsciously mimicking his eyebrow movements at the same time. 'Did you really expect me to fall at your feet in undying gratitude for such a magnanimous proposal?'

He laughed, moving her temperature into the white-hot bracket.

'I've already learnt that nothing about you will ever be that easy, Kate.' His hand rubbed his chin as he watched her thoughtfully. 'I do find it rather intriguing that it's the marriage proposal you appear to find offensive, whereas the—mm—dubious alternative at least produced a little soul-searching. It seemed a perfectly sensible solution to me.'

'For you, maybe,' she snapped back, angry at his unemotional, *sensible* acceptance of something he had found abhorrent to contemplate only a week ago. 'Do forgive my failure to be flattered, Greg—but yes, I did find the—dubious alternative preferable. That at least was honest.'

'And what would be dishonest about us being married? There'd be nothing hole-in-the-corner about us being together. We're both adult enough not to expect any more than either of us can give. I can give you financial security. Your family would be well cared for, Kate. I know that's important to you.'

Kate's temper left her as suddenly as it arrived. She felt as if she had spent the last few days on a roller-coaster and now it was time to disembark.

This mess wasn't Greg's fault. How could she blame him for acting true to his nature? It wasn't in him to lie to her about his feelings. He liked her, respected her, wanted her enough to put aside his distaste for the marital state to offer her what he thought she needed—the security of a wedding ring.

How wrong he was, though! What security could there be in

a desire which could wane as astonishingly quickly as it had risen? However tempted she was by his proposal, and deep down inside her a voice cried out against her more practical decision, Kate was no gambler. So she attempted to reason with him.

'What about you, Greg? You don't really want to marry me, do you?'

'No,' he agreed with unflattering placidity. 'Although I have to admit it does have its attractions.' The predatory glint in his eye did not need clarification. Kate drew back physically, even as her body wilfully responded to the message he was sending. 'But it is, I think, the only way out of this impasse. I'd be rather loath to lose your father's respect. He's a fine man, and too principled to look the other way when we become lovers.'

'Why is his respect so important to you?' Kate could not help her curiosity. 'You don't normally care what people think of you.' His face closed against her, but she persisted, some inner sense telling her it was important. 'Is it because of that man you said Dad reminded you of? Was it . . . your own father?'

A muscle worked in his jaw, but at least the brows stayed at half-mast! He exhaled on a long, hissing breath.

'Yes,' he admitted tightly, his reluctance plain to see. 'He died when I was twelve. Save your pity, Kate,' he added harshly at her indrawn gasp. 'It was a long time ago. And he had ceased to be my father a long time before that.'

'And your mother?' she probed gently, her soft heart going out to the lonely child he must have been.

'What's this, Kate? Psychoanalysis time?' Greg snapped, layers of ice frosting his eyes.

'No,' Kate retorted mildly, for she knew he was hurting. 'It's the reason I can't marry you. You only want to share a bed, Greg. To me, marriage means sharing a life.'

'Then what's your solution, Kate?' he asked, not attempting to deny her claim.

She looked at him sharply, bewildered, her temper again having drained her of the ability to think straight.

'What?'

'You've rejected an affair, and marriage. What do you

propose we do?'

She swallowed hard. 'We forget it. Stop it now. It's the only way, Greg! You must see that!' she implored, almost begged his understanding, her previous anger giving way to distress out of all proportion to the logical arguments she had thought out all week.

'And how do you stop this, Kate?' He was before her in the blink of an eye, lifting her head to meet his lowering mouth.

'No . . .' was all she had a chance to say before her words were captured by his lips, his tongue. She sagged fully against him, feeling the magic she had longed for begin to rise again, the woodsy flavour of his aftershave dulling her survival instincts.

'And this . . .' his teeth captured her earlobe, nipping with exquisite sensitivity. 'How do you propose to stop this, Kate?' His hands refused to still, roaming up and down, over and around her until she could not stop the moan of desire which brought his mouth back to hers.

'If you know of a way to stop this craving, then tell me now, before I lose my sanity completely!' He held her at arm's length. 'There's only one way I know, Kate. Is that what you want?'

She stared at him wordlessly, not even questioning any more his power to reduce her to such a state of trembling anticipation. When he held her, touched her, all she knew was that she did not want him to stop. Ever!

'I could take you now, Kate, here, on the office floor where anyone could walk in at any time, and you wouldn't be able to lift a finger to stop me!' He shook her slightly, his fingers biting into her upper arms. 'Would you, Kate?' he demanded thickly, his pupils so dilated she caught her own spellbound reflection in them.

She tried to shake her head in denial of his challenge, but she knew, deep down, that he spoke no less than the truth.

She turned away from him in shame, rebuttoning her blouse with trembling fingers, but even that simple task proved to be beyond her. With a muttered imprecation, Greg pushed her hands aside and completed the task. Kate did not have the time to wonder at the satisfaction she felt as she saw his fingers, too, begin to shake as they inadvertently brushed the soft mound of her breast.

'I've tried every alternative over the past two years, Kate. They don't work.' His voice was harsh, a note of resentment telling her that he didn't like the situation any more than she did, but his hands dropped to her shoulders, gently kneading away the rigidity in her body. 'Are you really so innocent that you believe we can continue working together with this—obsession unresolved?' His lips moved in the semblance of a smile. 'I had a bad enough time before I tasted your sweetness, Kate, but now . . . now I know you feel the same . . .' his eyes roamed possessively over her.

'Then I'll have to leave.'

'No! If you're thinking of taking Walsh's offer seriously, you can forget it!'

It was crazy. He was crazy. And he was infecting her with the same insanity. She could feel herself weakening under his seductive touch, his words stirring her, destroying her well thought out arguments against becoming further involved with him.

He didn't really want marriage; he had made that plain enough. And whatever it was that had made him so cynical towards marriage had certainly not vanished in the few days he had been away. No, what he wanted was a legalised affair. Some way to be able to sleep with her while retaining the respect of her father.

Marriage, to Kate, was something sacred, something she felt needed total commitment from both parties, if it was to stand the test of time. And she had no intention of becoming just another statistic in the divorce court.

She did not trouble to refute his earlier comment. In all honesty, she couldn't. However much it shamed her to admit it, if only to herself, Greg could probably make love to her in a public park. When he touched her the outside world ceased to exist. And it was getting worse. He had chosen the right word—obsession.

If she continued working with him they would become lovers with the same inevitability as night followed day. The only sane solution was for her to resign.

'Greg, it's the only way.'

He let go of her so abruptly she almost fell.

'You can't leave,' he told her flatly, his brows as low as she had ever seen them. But she was unconcerned with his moods now. She had to make him see reason. For if the time ever came that they did make love, she was very afraid she would become addicted in a way he would never allow.

'I don't want to, Greg.' Her expression was earnest. 'I love working here—with you. But you're right, we can't carry on like this.' It would be hard to leave. It would be even harder to find another job like this, but, even at a lower salary, it had to be better than facing this temptation day in, day out.

'The ink's not even dry on the contract you've just signed, Kate.'

He took her totally unawares. The harsh, cold words took a while to sink in, but once they did, she looked at him mutely, waiting for him to tell her that he didn't mean what she thought. But he said nothing, just watched her through those cold, dissecting eyes and waited for her to react. She took a deep wavering breath to alleviate her growing unease.

'What are you saying?'

Greg gestured towards the papers sitting with such assumed innocence on his desktop—a contract Kate had indeed signed less than an hour ago. It had all been straightforward enough when he had explained it to her. She had agreed to stay in his employment for the next two years, or until such time as Callum was in a position to begin repaying the loan Greg had given him. It had seemed a reasonable enough precaution considering the amount of money involved, and Kate had had no qualms about signing it.

But now, with his eyes boring into hers with such cold intent, she knew she had very possibly made the biggest mistake of her life. He lost no time in confirming it.

'You, more than anyone, should know how I feel about contracts, Kate.'

Yes, she knew. Contracts had to be carried out to the letter. Kate was visited by the sudden memory of a well-known firm who had reneged on a contract with Courtney's. Greg had taken them to court, spending far more on lawyers' fees than the contract was actually worth. And he had won. Kate's head bowed with the weight of comprehension.

'You're not going to let me go, are you?' It was a statement rather than a question. How could she have so quickly forgotten his capacity for ruthlessness, how swiftly he pounced when his mind was made up? She could have been a new company he was proposing to draw into his empire for all the emotion he was displaying, but, in a strange moment's empathy with him, Kate sensed he hated having to coerce her in this fashion—but not enough to make him desist. It was almost as if he wanted her to dislike him!

Watching him now, catching the steely determination written plainly on his face, she knew she had been adroitly manipulated into this position. And he was not about to allow her to escape.

It was then, with a clawing of horror in the pit of her stomach, that she remembered what else had been in that contract. Her home!

'So that's why . . .' she breathed deeply to offset the numbing resignation stealing over her as comprehension dawned. White-faced, she challenged him. 'That's why you talked Dad into taking the loan!' Greg stiffened at the bleak accusation and opened his mouth to speak, then abruptly changed his mind and remained silent. 'You want to know the really funny part, Greg?' Her voice began to shake. 'I'm the one who told Dad to trust you. Told him that I'd never met a more honourable man with whom to do business.' She took a perverse pleasure in the way he flinched. 'So. Either I come to your bed or you take our home away, is that it?'

'I don't much care why you come to my bed, Kate, just so long as you do. And there's no need to play the bloody martyr. You can't deny you want me too!'

'I haven't.'

'No. But then you haven't been aware of it for as long as I have. It eats away at you, Kate, until you'll do practically anything to satisfy the craving.'

Kate retreated inside herself, fearful that he was telling her no more than the truth, but too proud, too accountable to herself to give in.

'You wouldn't go that far . . .'

He smiled tightly. 'Have you ever known me to bluff, Kate?'

'No.' Any hope she had left swiftly died. 'No—your threats are carried out as dutifully as your promises.'

If she were to leave, Greg would be free to demand repayment immediately. His only reason for postponing payments—that Kate should not be distracted from her duties by money worries—would have ceased to exist.

'Am I to take it that my respect means nothing to you?'

He eyed her quizzically. 'I rather thought I'd already lost that.' His shrugging acceptance of her hard contempt showed her just how little he cared. 'Yes, it means something. But not so much as the other things you offer so—enticingly.'

Her stubborn chin lifted. 'If I keep to the letter of that contract there's nothing you can do.'

'You can try.' She heard the taunting note in his clipped voice. So he thought he was so bloody irresistible that she wouldn't be able to help herself, huh? She would show him!

'I don't like being manipulated, Greg. I'll be in my office if you want . . . need anything.'

The brief movement of his lips indicated that he had noticed her slip, but thankfully he did not take advantage.

Kate gathered the remains of her dignity around her like a cloak, and left. The thought of continuing to work for Gregory Courtney in these circumstances was likely to have her escorted, frothing at the mouth, to the nearest psychiatric institution before the end of the month—let alone two years! But she would do it.

Anything rather than surrender so unconditionally to his underhand scheming.

CHAPTER FIVE

SHEER rage was enough to sustain Kate through the next few hours. She raced through a mountain of paperwork at breakneck speed, work which would normally have taken at least a couple of days if done with her usual meticulousness. But, as always when she was in the grip of temper, her mind concentrated so fiercely on the task in hand, nothing was allowed to impinge, nothing could battle through the invisible shield she had erected.

Until Greg reminded her that he had been invited to her home for the evening. She had forgotten. Had kept a firm hold on her anger, knowing she could not afford to let it drain away until she was out of his orbit. She could not hold it any longer. Normally it only lasted the few seconds necessary for her to get the words off her chest and was gone the next instant. She accepted his offer of a lift home with abnormally bad grace which only served to fuel his diabolical sense of humour.

It was during the journey home that Kate realised just how hard a task she had set for herself.

In the close confines of his car, she found his proximity overpowering, the sure movement of his hands on the steering wheel a sharp reminder of how those same hands had touched her skin with the same sure skill.

How could she have misjudged him so badly? She had thought him so honourable—and not without cause. Countless times she had witnessed business associates shake his hand in the sure knowledge that they could trust his word. Even now, she could not imagine him treating anyone else in the same manner he had her. Oh, he had always been hard, blunt, but totally straightforward. He gave his word and kept it, no matter what. But then he had always used all available information to forge the best deal possible for

Courtney's.

It was no wonder he had been so insistent for her to confide in him. And, like the naïve idiot she was, she had poured all her troubles into his lap. He must have thought it was his birthday! He certainly didn't waste a second in following through!

Even on their last evening together, reeling from his lovemaking, she had felt grateful that he had the decency not to lure her into his bed by using the charm she knew he possessed. How he must have laughed when she told him she appreciated his honesty! But she had.

Had he gone about her seduction in the normal manner, it was perfectly possible she would have fallen in love with him. It was difficult enough to remain aloof as it was. All the ingredients were certainly present—the undoubted physical attraction which had always been in the back of her mind, her warmer feelings towards him after that awful scene with Toby Marchant, her gratitude on behalf of her family, her respect for him personally.

Why, why did he have the integrity to warn her against falling in love with him when that could only be to his benefit, then immediately scheme in such a manner to prevent her taking the only practical steps to stop any such catastrophe happening? And why her, for heaven's sake?

Why should anyone go to such lengths to obtain something so freely available elsewhere? Kate would not have been human had she not realised her looks appealed to a great many men. But she was also the first to admit that they weren't outstanding enough to inspire a grand passion. Surely a man of Greg's stature would have no difficulty in attracting the very best that womanhood could offer?

And she did not, for one moment, think he had been nurturing a secret unrequited love for her these past two years. He had been very frank on that score!

He was so totally out of her orbit in every way. Socially, financially, his whole concept of relationships was alien to her.

And she still wanted him.

It was beyond her tired brain to decipher all the whys and

wherefores. She only knew Greg would not give up. And she could not give in. Stalemate.

At least she knew if it came to a last resort, she could count on her family's support. Even if it meant losing their home, everything they had worked for all their lives, they would give it up immediately rather than see her suffer. She prayed it would not come to that.

Watching her father that evening, Kate knew it would be the hardest thing she would ever be called upon to do. Greg caught that thought—and the bitterness which accompanied it. It was there in the lowering of his brows, the thinning of his lips—and in his eyes, another message was plain. They would become lovers!

Alissa had gone to town on the celebration, as only she could. The dining-table was groaning under the weight of the food Kate's young brothers were eyeing with undisguised hunger.

Terry, fortunately, provided a buffer. He knew better than to bring one of his blonde playmates to Callum McNaught's home. Kate's father was not exactly Victorian in his attitude to sex—more like puritanical! While he would not dream of interfering in Terry's private life, neither would he tolerate any 'goings-on' under his roof.

Greg, who should have stood out like a sore thumb as being outside the family circle, endeared himself at once by presenting a case of wine to Alissa and a crate of beer to Callum. 'To help the party along,' he said. Then he sat talking computer language to Ian and Andy and became the hero of the hour when he discreetly presented the two boys with a special pass to Edgbaston cricket ground. How he had discovered the two were cricket fanatics, Kate did not know. But she was no longer capable of being surprised at anything he did.

Yet again the conversation in the McNaught household looked like being centred on Gregory Courtney.

For one chagrined moment, as their eyes met across the room, Kate took the time to wonder how her family would react if she were to produce one of her infamous tantrums. Stamping her feet and howling her eyes out at full volume held a particular appeal. Unfortunately this was not the time to regress to childhood. She was going to need all her wits about her to emerge from this fiasco unscathed. And no doubt Greg would interpret such a proceeding as an indication of surrender. If he even noticed! But just then Callum was issuing his inevitable open-handed invitation to 'drop in any time you're passing, son.'

Kate already knew there would be no escaping Greg's presence. At work, at home—he would be wherever she was. He had the perfect excuse of consulting Callum and Terry about the new business.

Worse was to come.

About half-way through the evening's festivities, Kate noticed her mother slip unobtrusively from the room. With a feeling of apprehension, Kate quietly followed her a few minutes later. She could not have said why she was concerned, but there had been something in Alissa's manner which did not quite ring true.

Kate found her mother lying across her bed, sobbing as if her heart would break.

'Mom! Mom, please—what is it?'

Kate never could bear to see her mother cry. She was such a strong woman, the backbone of the family. For her to break down in such a manner could only mean something devastating had occurred.

'Oh, Katherine! I'm so sorry—I didn't mean to spoil the party for you. This is so silly . . .!'

'But why, Mom?' Kate gathered her mother into her arms. 'Everything's fine now,' she lied.

'That's why I'm being so silly, Katherine. The relief . . .' She stifled a convulsive sob. 'Oh, Katherine—I thought I'd lost him! If your Gregory hadn't . . .' Alissa stopped abruptly, biting her lip, and controlled her tears through sheer force of will. Kate's forebodings grew tenfold.

'What do you mean, Mom?'

'I shouldn't be bothering you with this, Katherine. Not now. This is a happy day . . .'

'Mom!'

Kate was not Callum's daughter for nothing. Alissa took

one look at the angle of her chin, noted the determination in her eyes and conceded defeat.

'Your father was going to leave us, Katherine,' she admitted finally in a hushed voice. 'That day—you know, when I called you home from work?' Kate nodded. She had been so worried herself, she hadn't stopped to consider how out of character it was for her mother to fall to pieces. That only happened at times like now, when the crisis was over. 'I found a packed suitcase under the bed—that's why I panicked. He . . . he'd been saying for weeks that he couldn't stand taking money from you any longer. He said that if—if you wouldn't agree to the second mortgage then . . . then we'd be better off without him. That you were the head of the household now, that there was no place for him. I—Katherine, you know how he is when his mind's made up. We'd have lost him, Katherine, without your Gregory.'

Years later, Kate was able to pinpoint that moment as the time she subconsciously admitted defeat. Cradling her mother's head on her shoulder, she knew her last resort had been blocked. The McNaughts could pull through anything together—but Kate could not be the catalyst to pull them apart.

Even so, her capitulation took a further two weeks.

Greg did not touch her, did not speak to her about anything but business. He merely existed—everywhere.

He took full advantage of Callum's invitation to drop in. The one evening she escaped to the local pub with Terry, Greg turned up half an hour later. Robbed of any respite from his disturbing presence, Kate had no opportunity to shore up her defences against the potent attraction which was dragging her into a mire of sexual craving. Her dilemma was acute.

She was normally such a calm, level-headed person. She had never wished for the moon, had no burning ambition, had no need of bright lights in order to enjoy herself. These new sensations were so totally outside her experience, she had no idea how to even begin to overcome the hunger which was fast becoming intolerable. The fierce yearning to recreate the magic they had so briefly shared was balanced only by her own innate sense of self-worth. She had a right to expect her decisions to be respected.

She felt as she imagined an alcoholic would, faced every second with a bottle of whisky in full tempting view, knowing that by merely reaching out a hand she could satisfy the gnawing craving. For a little while, at least.

Her body turned traitor at every look, at every thought. She made so many mistakes at work, Greg was forced to comment about it. After all her efforts to reason with him had met with abject failure, she listened to his patiently understanding lecture with growing resentment.

'So fire me!' she blazed at him when he had finished.

'I intend to, Kate,' he replied, his sardonic expression not quite overcoming the husky note in his voice when he added, 'Something along the lines of spontaneous combustion!' And he continued his waiting game.

On the following Friday Kate finally cracked under the strain. Her mother took one look at her flushed face and ordered her back to bed.

Kate was too exhausted to argue. Her throat burned, her head was drumming a tattoo, and her eyelids were simply too heavy to remain open. She slept throughout the day. She was barely aware of the comings and goings through her bedroom, the doctor's visit, her mother's constant presence, or of Greg's visit later that day. Her fever broke in the night, but Kate slept on.

When she did finally awake properly, she was totally disorientated, and a little light-headed. Her throat was parched, but a more immediate, not to say urgent necessity was a visit to the bathroom.

The house was unnaturally silent as she made her way there, hanging on to the wall for support, but Kate knew she was not alone. Her mother had very firm ideas when it came to sick members of the McNaught family. Pampering was the number one priority. She stared longingly at the bath. She felt so stale and sticky. A brief look in the mirror had been enough to inform her that the only colour in her face was the freckles standing out in stark contrast to the pallor of her skin. Her eyes were almost transparent.

Acting on impulse, she turned the bath taps on full, with the ridiculous idea that perhaps she could be in and out of the bath before anyone heard the water running. But she heard the footsteps pounding up the stairs before she had even straightened up. She turned with resignation towards the door, trying to summon a little energy to do battle with her mother.

But it was not Alissa who exploded into the bathroom. It was Greg! Kate stared at him, wide-eyed and totally defenceless.

'Where's my mother?' she demanded, annoyed that her voice was no more than a croak.

'She's gone out with your father and the boys. She needed some fresh air.' He took a complete, thorough inventory of her—tangled red waves, shadowed eyes, bloodless lips and, naturally, the thin apricot cotton nightdress she had worn since she was a teenager. Kate would have screamed had she possessed the energy. Greg was dressed casually in a thin grey sweater and slacks and looked as fresh as a spring morning! 'I offered to babysit,' he added at Kate's desolate look. 'How are you feeling?'

'I'm fine.'

'You don't look it.' He stepped forward to place a cool hand against her forehead. Kate jerked back out of his reach. 'Dammit, Kate! I'm not in the habit of jumping on sick women!' His eyes blazed angrily.

'I know.' Kate was immediately contrite. She also knew she did not have the strength to argue. 'Please, Greg, just let me have a bath.' She bent over to turn off the taps as the bathroom filled with steam.

Greg sighed impatiently, raking his fingers through his dark hair as he frowned at her.

'I don't think a bath is on the list of instructions your mother left.'

A ghost of a smile touched Kate's lips. 'Don't tell me! Chicken soup, fruit juice, aspirins and sleep.' She thought it prudent not to mention the hugs.

'She was worried about you.'

Kate looked up in surprise. He sounded almost defensive.

'I know.—I'm not griping. But I am going to have a bath before she gets home and stops me . . . So——' She looked pointedly at the door. His eyes narrowed at the stubborn set of her jaw, then, amazingly, he grinned. It was just as well Kate was in no state to appreciate the difference it made to his whole face. With a conspiratorial wink, he carefully looked over his shoulder and lowered his voice.

'OK, I'll get you a robe—if you promise not to let your mother know.'

'Are you kidding? It'd be more than my life's worth!'

Kate let out a long breath as he left her. For once, happily devoid of any sexual feelings towards him, it now seemed she had to battle against the urge to be friendly. He reappeared within seconds, handing her a long navy winter dressing-gown.

'I am under the strictest of instructions to ensure you don't catch a chill.' He stilled her objections before they could form. 'I'll go and get the soup ready.'

'Right.'

'Kate?' She looked up at him as he wavered on the threshold and caught an uncharacteristic uncertainty in his expression. 'I——Forget it. Don't lock the door. And if you're not out in five minutes, I shall come in and get you.'

She took three minutes, then defiantly yielded to the temptation to wash her hair. She had very nearly finished when the shower spray was unceremoniously yanked out of her hand.

'You little fool! Why didn't you ask for help?'

'Because I don't need it. Will you give me that back? I'm getting soap in my eyes.'

Greg went one better. Very gently he tipped her head forwards over the basin and washed away the shampoo suds, then carefully wrapped her hair in a towel.

'Don't say a word, Kate!' he muttered gruffly as he lifted her into his arms to carry her downstairs to the kitchen.

The table was already laid. A bowl of steaming chicken soup was placed before her, and under Greg's watchful eyes she began to eat. Strangely, there was no self-consciousness. Never in a million years could she have imagined sitting easily across a table from him dressed in an old dressing-gown, devoid of make-up, feeling—cared for. Would married life be like this? The thought was seductive—more so to Kate than the sensual sparks which flew between them. It was also too dangerous to deal with when her defence mechanisms were not in full working order.

Greg cleared away the dishes the second she finished and ushered her into the lounge to sit before the fire he had recently laid. Although they were at the beginning of summer there was a nip in the air today, and Greg was apparently taking Alissa McNaught's words to heart.

'Let's get that hair dry before your mother gets home!' he ordered brusquely, and whipped the towel off her head before she had a chance to speak. He looked helplessly at the thick dripping tendrils. 'Do you have a hair-dryer or something?'

'In my room.'

Kate smothered a grin as she heard him run hurriedly up the stairs. What she wouldn't give for her mother's ability to turn him into a helpless dithering male! She knew the lecture he had been given. Number three on the care and recuperation of McNaught children—irrespective of their age. Instructions to be followed to the letter—or else! It seemed Gregory Courtney had finally met his match! He might be master of the boardroom, but in this house everyone danced to Alissa's tune, whether they knew it or not. It was comforting to know Greg was possessed of an Achilles' heel after all.

Kate insisted on drying her own hair. Although she was still generally weak, the warm bath and hot soup had restored some strength.

She did not think of asking Greg to leave. For one thing, it was doubtful he would even listen to her. And for another, Alissa would be very distressed to learn that her poor ewe lamb had been left unattended. So she sat on the rug before the fire and tended to her hair, only gradually becoming conscious that Greg was watching her every movement.

'Let me do that!'

'There's no . . .' Too late. He took the brush from her

clenched fingers and turned her so that she was sitting at his feet.

The swift sudden upsurge of desire as his fingers gently untangled her waves took her completely by surprise. Her heightened senses must have communicated themselves to him, for he stopped abruptly and slowly propelled her round to face him, tilting her chin the easier to read her expression.

'Do I frighten you so much, Kate?'

'Sometimes.' She licked her dry lips. 'The way you make me feel. It's . . .'

'It's mutual. I don't like it any more than you do, Kate. But you can't deny it's there. And it's time we dealt with it.'

Her lids drifted down to hide the slumbrous sensuality she could feel stealing over her.

'You can't win, you know.' Absently his hands roamed the outer edges of her face. Gently he began tugging her towards him and trailed the lightest of kisses along her jaw.

'No . . . It's—I can't!'

'Ssh, it's all right, Kate. Just a taste . . . I need just a taste . . .'

'Please!'

'Give in, Kate!' he urged huskily as his mouth continued to press whispering kisses down the long line of her vulnerable throat, setting up shivers of delight throughout her nervous system.

Vainly she tried to fight off the lassitude pushing her further into his embrace. How could it feel so right to be held in his arms when she knew it was so wrong?

But Greg gave her no chance to gather any scant reserves of will she possessed. She became easy prey to the hot, sweet lips scouring a sensitised path across her jaw down to the delicate bones at the base of her throat, where he buried his face for one long moment before journeying back to claim her lips.

Kate was lost in his gentleness. Unconsciously her hands drifted beneath the thin stuff of his sweater and became engrossed in their journey of discovery across his hair-roughened chest. His hoarse groan only added to the magic he was creating with his lips and hands. She was not frightened by the evidence of his arousal this time, but gloryed in it, as he lay down beside her on the carpet, moving to cover her body with his own.

'Greg, please . . .!' Her mumbled entreaties for a release from the growing ache inside her were lost in his mouth.

'Kate. Sweet Kate . . .'

She gave even as she received, covering his face with open-mouthed kisses. She lost all sense of time and place . . . lost all the reasons why she must keep her distance from him. Wanting, needing desperately to put an end to this intolerable craving . . .

The startled gasps from the doorway did not impinge on her consciousness, but the loosening of Greg's hold did.

'Greg? What . . .?' The words died in her throat as her love-dazed eyes were captured in the misery of her father's stricken face!

Greg shielded her partly clad body from the dismayed, transfixed stares of her parents. Carefully he pulled her robe back into place, staring at her with a disturbing intensity she missed, everything in her focused on the man she loved more than any other in the world—her father.

'Dad . . .?' Ignoring her trembling plea, Callum McNaught stood as if carved from stone, his fierce pride in his daughter as ashes in his mouth. He could not even bring himself to look at her.

Satisfied that she was now presentable, Greg rose and, very gently, as if she were the frailest of creatures, he pulled her to her feet, an arm clasped firmly around her waist as he faced Callum.

'Callum, you'll have to forgive us,' he began quietly, sombrely. 'Your daughter has just agreed to marry me.' He smiled a little sheepishly at the arrested expressions of delight from the duo in the doorway, but his iron grip manacled Kate to his side as she sagged. 'I've been trying to persuade her for some time—and in the excitement of the moment,' he grimaced ruefully, 'I'm afraid things got a little out of hand.'

Kate had been feeling as if she was taking part in a particularly nasty nightmare until Greg's comment about marriage.

About to deny it with all the force left to her, she caught her father's pain-filled eyes and choked on the words.

This was it, then. Greg had won.

How could she not agree to the one thing which could banish the misery from her father's face—to the one thing which would allow him to accept Greg's money—to the one thing to keep her family together?

'Daddy?' The childish term slipped from her lips as if she had been catapulted back to the days when a smile from her father could brighten the dullest of days. His arms opened wide to receive her. And Alissa finally found her voice as she joined the embrace.

'Well, I know I insisted Greg took care of you, but I never imagined this was what he had in mind!'

'Callum?'

Greg and Callum took stock of each other. Despite his being caught in such a highly compromising situation, Greg's natural authority was undiminished. A firm handshake brought their silent confrontation to a mutually satisfied end. Tactfully, Kate's parents then withdrew to allow Greg time alone with his very new fiancée.

Swallowing the bitter taste of defeat, Kate moved like an automaton to the windows, focused but unseeing on the surrounding view. Shoulders slumped in dejection, forehead absorbing the refreshing cool of the windowpane, she inwardly flinched at the soft touch of Greg's hands on her upper arms; soothing, stroking, as if to imbue her with his own strength.

'I'm sorry it had to be this way, Kate.' The liquid tones flowed over her, his sincerity unmistakable, but Kate was beyond any comfort he could give. Shrugging off his hands, she turned to him with barely concealed bitterness.

'You're sorry? Hah!' The short harsh laugh she gave was an accusation in itself. 'You know, Greg, that could be almost funny if it weren't so pathetic. You can take your damned false apologies and lock them away with the empty promises and lies you so honourably refuse to use to placate me!' Despite the ragged edge to her voice, her confused exhaustion lent her the impetus to refuse to bow to his quelling glare. For once the metallic glitter of his eyes had no effect on her.

'I suppose I deserved that.' His head bowed slightly in acknowledgement of her jibe, but his impassive features remained carved in granite. His eyes were watchful, intent on her reaction as if he were readying himself for whatever she might do.

'Why me, Greg? There are thousands of women out there who would gladly give you what you want.'

'I dare say we'll find the answer to that on our wedding night!' For a moment he sounded as weary as Kate felt. She shook her head slowly in disbelief at his callous tone.

'This must be some kind of bad dream!'

'It's real enough, Kate. Just resign yourself to it.'

'What kind of man are you, Greg?'

'The kind who gets his own way!' His voice was as clipped and cold as the steely eyes regarding her.

'And now there's nothing to stop you, is there?'

He hesitated, breathing deeply. 'One thing. There is one thing which would stop me, Kate.' He spoke slowly, spacing his words with great care as he moved closer to tower over her, his long hands cupping her face, darkening eyes boring into hers as she waited with bated breath for the get-out clause. 'Look at me, Kate! Look me in the eye and tell me you don't want me! Then I'll let you go.' He laughed shortly, mirthlessly. 'I'll even set things right with your father. So tell me, Kate! Tell me you don't want me. Tell me you hate the feel of my hands on your body. Tell me you find me repulsive! Tell me, Kate!'

It should have been easy. Kate felt the lie rise to her lips, but as she opened her mouth the falsehood stuck in her throat. Pinned, mesmerised by the sensual impact of unwavering grey eyes, feeling his clean breath hot on her face, inhaling his familiar scent, she knew the denial was lost. In one short breath she became a spitting bundle of fury, two weeks of pent-up frustration bursting forth in glorious rage.

'Damn you, Greg! Damn you to hell!' She caught him totally off guard with the suddenness of her attack. She pummelled his chest furiously with clenched fists, even slapping him backhandedly across his face until he pinned her arms behind her back in sheer self-defence, and held her close until her fury had burnt itself out.

He held her head cradled against his chest, tenderly stroking her hair. 'Poor Kate,' he murmured softly. For a brief span of time she lay quiescent against him. Her fury spent, she was drained of energy, swamped by an unaccountable relief that the battle was finally over. Even if she had lost.

She had had to be strong and independent for so long that the temptation to hand over all her burdens was overwhelming.

Greg would take his responsibilities seriously. Would it be so bad to give in to this debilitating weakness to accept what he offered? To bury herself in his passion without longing for his love? Love? Where had that idea come from?

The temptation died as swiftly as it had arisen. Yes, she could fall in love with him. Very easily, in fact, if she did not guard herself against it—as he had warned her. With an instinct so clear as to be almost palpable, she knew that somewhere deep inside Greg was a human being as emotionally vulnerable as herself; so scared of being hurt or rejected, he refused to lay his feelings open to attack. Buried so deep, it would take little short of a miracle to bring them to the surface.

Oh, yes, she could fall in love with him—if she wanted to commit emotional suicide. Kate was neither a fool nor a masochist.

No. The battle might be over, but there was still a war to be fought. She had to continue fighting him, had to try to despise him. There was no other way if she was to retain any pretence of self-respect.

Decision made, she pulled jerkily out of his arms.

'I'm going back to bed,' she said. He smiled slightly at her polite tone with no trace of his usual mockery.

'Very well, Kate. I'll let you run away for now.'

'I'm quite incapable of running. Besides,' she looked up into his softened face, 'you've left me nowhere to run.'

He stiffened at her bitterly weary accusation, his face

becoming an unreadable mask.

'I'm glad you appreciate that,' he intoned heavily. 'It won't be so bad, Kate, I promise.'

She turned at the door, her whole body crying a negation of the events which had taken her over.

'You said once you wouldn't make promises you couldn't keep, Greg. Don't start now.'

CHAPTER SIX

'THANK heaven that's over!' Kate's husband heaved a sigh of relief on returning to the car, after removing the decorations her brothers had seen fit to plaster all over the once gleaming Mercedes. Tight-lipped, Greg leaned back in his seat as Kate made no effort to reply.

The normal dark grey business suit she was used to had been replaced by a lighter grey which had the effect of making him look even more devastatingly attractive than ever, she thought with complete detachment. She had chosen to be married in a cream tight-waisted suit, the colour unfortunately underlining her too-pale complexion.

She had followed orders and smiled dutifully throughout the small reception her parents had insisted on giving. As Sam and Marie Goodis had been Greg's only guests, Kate had been able to persuade her parents that it would be unkind to overwhelm Greg with their huge family contingent at this early stage. The truth was much more simple: she knew she could not have borne the sincere congratulations her hordes of relatives would no doubt have heaped upon her.

She had also adamantly overruled her parents' objections to a civil ceremony. There was no way Kate could have uttered the beautiful words of the marriage service, not in these circumstances. Greg had had the gall to attempt to persuade her to change her mind. Sheer bloody-mindedness! she had raged at him. How he could even contemplate swearing those kind of vows was beyond her.

For once, Kate won—backed by her father, however reluctantly, when she declared how hypocritical it would be to use the Church for her own ends when she was not a regular attendant. Callum McNaught was not the man to deny a principle, however painful it proved to live with.

89

Only one portion of the ceremony remained clear in Kate's mind. The rest was a mere blur. The moment Greg had slipped the plain gold band on her finger. He had stared at it intently for several seconds with fiercely possessive satisfaction before placing his cool lips upon her unresponsive mouth.

'If you want to sulk for the rest of the journey, Kate, I suggest you get in the back and try to get some sleep,' Greg bit out tersely, dragging her mind back to the present. He was patently displeased by her pale features and shadowed eyes. 'You look as if you could use it!'

'I have never sulked in my life!' The retort sprang automatically to her lips. It had become a point of honour not to allow his sneers to pass unchallenged. 'If I have anything to say, then I say it!'

'Yes,' he murmured, shooting her a dry glance, 'I had noticed.' He caught her resisting hand in his and raised it to his lips to press an open-mouthed kiss into the palm. Kate shuddered. Apart from that one cool kiss at the register office, this was the first time he had touched her with any intimacy since that dreadful débâcle at her home. 'My apologies, sweet Kate. It is indeed my good fortune to possess such a paragon among women!'

Mocking devil! And Kate had spent the best part of the morning contemplating the shocking idea that she might possibly have fallen in love with him! At that precise moment she could not truthfully say she even desired him. He was a stranger, a cold-eyed, remote stranger who, in a painfully short time, would be taking her to bed!

Without another word, she removed herself to the back of the car and wearily closed her eyes. She had never felt so tired in her life.

The past few weeks had taken quite a toll. She had lost weight, her cheekbones stood out a little too prominently in her pale face. Her eyes, the mirrors of her eagerness and zest for life, had dulled.

Fortunately she had been able to put some of the blame on her short illness, but her mother naturally hit on the truth.

'Bridal jitters!' she announced firmly when Kate once

complained of her lack of energy.

Oh, yes, jittery was the word all right. Her nerves were shot to pieces. Insanity also sprang to mind, alongside suicidal. Anger was also a definite contender.

It almost consumed her at times, being forced to admit defeat in the face of Greg's clever conniving. And then—then there was the fear.

Not fear of Greg personally—nothing as simple as that. She feared the things he could make her feel, the things he forced her to acknowledge about herself. She feared the quick, uncontrollable flow of adrenalin whenever she caught sight of him.

But, for most of the short period of their engagement, Kate had embraced the fatalistic numbness which had anaesthetised her from the more disturbing aspects of her coming marriage. Except for one telling incident which slipped through, and had kept her tossing and turning for the past two nights, and which inevitably came back to haunt her anew.

Two nights ago Greg had escorted her to a party held in their honour by his best man, Sam Goodis. Kate had half-heartedly welcomed the opportunity to get to know Marie better.

'I always knew you'd get caught in the trap one day, lad!' Sam clapped Greg heartily on the back in welcome, his faint Yorkshire accent in evidence.

'Trap indeed!' his wife piped up in mock indignation. 'It's the women who are left in the cage, remember?'

But despite any traps or cages, it was obvious the couple were devoted to each other, and Kate happily allowed Marie to usher her upstairs to freshen up, with none of the reserve she normally felt with people she did not know well.

'This is a perfect house for parties,' Kate commented as they entered a large bedroom. 'So many rooms for little groups to congregate.'

'I know. I love it here,' Marie agreed with all the enthusiasm Kate had guessed she possessed. 'Sam thought I was crazy buying such a big house for the two of us, but I do adore parties! And I'm especially going to enjoy this one.' She grasped Kate's hand tightly, her warm face glowing with sincerity. 'I can't tell you how pleased I am that Greg has finally allowed someone like you to love him!' Hazel eyes brimming with tears of happiness did not see Kate's sudden frown at such an odd pronouncement. 'You'll be so good for him, Kate!'

'But you hardly know me, Marie,' Kate could not help but protest.

'Oh, bosh! Sam's talked a lot about you. And I know enough about people to sense that you're marrying the man, not the cheque book!' Marie clapped a hand over her mouth in dismay. 'Forgive me, Kate—I have a runaway tongue. But Greg is very special to me.'

'You've known him a long time, haven't you?' Kate said thoughtfully.

'Since he was a little lad of eight or nine. He didn't tell you?' Marie asked, noticing Kate's surprise.

'No—he . . . This was all a bit sudden, you know. He . . .' small white teeth worried at her lower lip, 'he doesn't talk much about his past.'

Marie sobered instantly. 'No—well, that's hardly surprising. We moved next door to the Courtneys when Sam and I first got married. Ben—that's Greg's father—and Sam used to work down the mines together. In fact, Sam saved Ben's life. There was a cave-in at the pit, you see.' Marie shuddered at what was patently a painful memory. 'Sam got Ben out, but the poor man's legs were crushed so badly he spent the rest of his life in a wheelchair. Believe me, I'll never be able to repay Greg for getting us out of that life.'

Kate sat silently, frightened to interrupt lest Marie stopped completely, and also a little frightened to have her continue, as her anger towards Greg softened with this fresh insight into his past.

'Greg worshipped Ben,' Marie continued, almost to herself. 'It used to break my heart to see that child caring for his father so diligently after the accident.'

'What happened to his mother?' Kate held her breath in suspense. She knew it could be nothing good, judging from

Greg's own reaction to the same question. Marie gave a guilty start.

'I shouldn't be talking like this, should I?'

'Please . . .' Kate urged, gripping Marie's hand tightly. 'I promise I won't tell him, but—I need to know!'

'Yes.' Marie's face softened, understanding Kate's urgency. 'Yes, you probably will. You haven't chosen an easy man to love, Kate. But he'll be worth everything you give him.

'Sharon Courtney was a first-class, top-notch, grade A selfish bitch! And Ben was besotted with her. The last I heard she was living in South Africa with her fourth or fifth husband—I lost count. Greg hasn't seen her since he packed his bags and walked out. He was sixteen. He always kept in touch with us, though, and as soon as he bought out Grainger he sent for Sam. He never forgets a favour——Hey, come on! Take that glum look off your face! This is a party!'

'Right.' It wasn't that hard for Kate to force a smile to her lips. Marie's gaiety was contagious. And she was so happy for the man Kate could see she looked upon as a son, Kate did not even contemplate disillusioning her with the real reason for this hastily arranged marriage.

And thankfully, there was no time to digest the information she had been given, except to subtly alter one of the words she had always used to describe Greg. 'Self-sufficient' disturbingly became 'lonely'.

'Kate—what a lovely dress! And what a figure!' Marie glanced down at her own ample proportions and grimaced comically. 'I console myself with the thought that Sam likes curves in a woman—and I've certainly got enough of those to keep him satisfied!'

They descended the stairs laughing. Kate was pleased Marie thought she was suitably attired. Greg had offered to buy her a new dress for the occasion, but Kate had refused, preferring to wear her favourite green, despite the bitter-sweet memories it provoked. Judging by the gathering arrivals, it appeared to be an 'anything goes' kind of party—some people sported jeans, others were in dinner jackets. Greg had steered a middle course of dark brown suede trousers, teamed with a lighter brown open-necked shirt.

The doorbell chimed as they were half-way down the staircase, announcing the arrival of yet more guests. Sam opened the door with a cheery 'hello'.

'Damn!' Marie startled Kate with the vehemence of her oath. She was becoming used to the older woman speaking in exclamations, but that 'damn' had sounded positively evil. 'Who the hell invited her?'

Kate followed the direction of Marie's malevolent glare to witness the arrival of a long-legged blonde, attractive in an obvious way, Kate decided, her green eyes glowing cattily. It did not take a mind-reader to work out the reason for her hostess's discomfort.

'One of Greg's exes, I presume?' she murmured drily, not wanting Marie to think she was upset.

'I'm afraid so.'

'How do you suppose she keeps that dress on, Marie?' Kate asked in genuine bewilderment. The scarlet silk revealed a lot more than it concealed.

'That, I suspect, is between her and her Maker! It looks as if she was sewn into the thing! I'm sorry about this, Kate. We certainly didn't invite her, but you can bet your life I'll find out who did and make mincemeat of him!' Kate spared a moment's sympathy for the unwitting culprit. Marie was looking quite fierce. She was rather touched that Marie should so soon feel friendly enough to become her champion. All her sympathy vanished, however, when she caught sight of Toby Marchant's taunting face as he took hold of the blonde's arm.

Kate studiously avoided them, until Greg made it impossible for her to do so by leading her over to the couple. Though he must have sensed her reluctance.

'Kate—darling, I'd like you to meet an old—friend of mine, Caroline Sterling. Caroline—my fiancée, Katherine McNaught.'

Kate was inspected and clearly dismissed as a nonentity with a limp handshake. Then the blonde wrapped herself around Greg and trilled up at him, 'More than old friends, darling. But I suppose I shouldn't say that in front of your—fiancée.'

His left eyebrow arched—just a touch. But enough to tell Kate he was amused rather than offended.

'No, Caroline, you shouldn't. But I don't suppose that will stop you,' he drawled.

'How well you know me!' Blue eyes sparkled brightly, clearly delighted. Toby Marchant, a little wiser these days, took one look at Kate's blank expression, and stepped back a pace. 'Tell me, darling, what have you been doing with yourself? It seems positively ages since we last—got together.' A brief suggestive look was thrown in Kate's direction.

'I've been persuading Kate to marry me, Caroline,' said Greg, firmly dissociating himself from the blonde's innuendoes. He underlined his intent by adding, 'And I would hate for you to undo all my good work.'

His eyes glinted a warning. Caroline pouted prettily, but loosened her hold on him, her scarlet talons now resting on his arm rather than cutting off his blood circulation.

'You must let me in on your secret, Katy.' Kate did not even wince at the hated nickname. Toby Marchant disappeared into the surrounding crowd. 'I've been trying to hook this gorgeous man for years.'

'Really?' Kate spoke for the first time, allowing her eyes to widen in simulated amazement. Caroline's insolent scrutiny of her slender body, obviously searching for signs of pregnancy, tipped her—just a little—over the edge. She totally ignored Greg's sharp intake of breath and slowly raised her left hand to smooth back an imaginary loose strand of hair, but making sure the diamonds surrounding the sparkling emerald in her engagement ring caught the light. It glinted mockingly. Then she leaned forward, lowering her voice to a conspiratorial whisper. 'Perhaps it's time to change the bait? Oh, do excuse me!' She glided past Greg. 'One of *my* old friends has just arrived!'

Blindly she made her way towards Terry, who was just introducing himself, and the girl at his side, to Marie.

'Hi, princess! This is Candy . . .'

'Cindy,' the small but perfectly formed blonde corrected

with the air of having done it so many times before. But she still gazed adoringly at Terry. 'I'll just go and freshen up. Don't go away now.'

'Gee, Terry, I'm glad to see you're gaining a little discrimination at last.' Terry looked blankly at Kate. 'This one can walk and talk at the same time!'

'OK, out with it, sweetheart!' he laughed. 'What's turned my sweet little princess into a sour-faced bitch?'

'Well, I wouldn't go that far,' Marie put in. 'But you do look a little frayed around the edges, dear.'

'Well, that's a relief!' Kate let out a heartfelt sigh, her uncertain temper evaporating in the warmth of her friend's concern. 'I thought at the very least, smoke would be pouring out of my ears!' She gave a disarmingly frank grin. 'Sorry, Tel, I'm sure Candy . . .'

'Cindy.'

'. . . is a very nice girl.'

'Oh, I do so hope you're wrong, princess!'

Their uninhibited laughter drew many curious glances, not the least of which was a narrow-eyed stare from the tall dark man coming up behind Kate.

'Care to share the joke?' Kate automatically stiffened as a heavy hand descended on her shoulder, Greg's deep voice vibrating over her head.

'Just telling our favourite gatecrasher tales,' Marie unknowingly fanned the flames with a mischievously guileless twinkle in her eye. 'Of course, we've never had a barracuda push her way in before . . .'

Kate's breath left her in a rush as she was drawn back against the full length of Greg's hard body.

'Are you by any chance referring to Caroline?' he asked drily.

'Well, if the teeth fit . . .' Marie sniffed. 'I don't like my guest of honour being upset.'

Whatever Greg was about to retort was lost in Terry's shout of laughter.

'Don't you worry your head about Kate, Marie. She might be a little lacking in the submission department, but when it comes to a knockout blow,' his eyes rolled graphically,

PLAY "LUCKY HEARTS" AND YOU COULD GET...

★ Exciting Harlequin Presents® novels—FREE
★ A gold-plated chain—FREE
★ A surprise mystery gift that will delight you—FREE

THEN CONTINUE YOUR LUCKY STREAK WITH A SWEETHEART OF A DEAL

'believe me, there's no contest! She has a temper you wouldn't believe!'

'Oh, good.' Marie positively beamed her approval before being whisked off to dance with Terry. Kate smiled fondly after them. Perhaps the evening wouldn't be so bad, after all.

'Walsh obviously knows when to beat a hasty retreat.'

'He's known me a long time.' She peeped up at him through the veil of her lashes, to gauge his mood, and hastily crossed her fingers behind her back! 'He knows the warning signals. A good lesson for any man to learn, don't you think?'

'Mmm,' Greg was noncommittal. He propelled her gently forward into the space cleared for dancing and turned her in his arms to move slowly in time to the music. Surprisingly, Kate found he danced well, and she managed to relax a little until his hard voice sounded in her ear.

'There's no cause for you to be jealous of Caroline, you know.'

Kate jerked back, but met his downward glance with unwavering steadiness. 'Who said anything about jealousy? I merely dislike being patronised.' Particularly by one of your alternatives, she added silently to herself, wondering if she really could be jealous. But surely that would mean . . .?

'I think I'd like some champagne.'

Greg stuck close to her for most of the evening, for which she was grateful. Except for Terry, these people were mainly Greg's friends, and, although Kate knew most of them through work, she did not feel totally comfortable with them in a social setting. So they danced, chatting with outward amiability whenever anyone came up to them, no one giving any indication that they saw through the masquerade she and Greg were enacting for their benefit. She was to become quite horrified at the ease with which the falsehoods fell from her lips.

She enjoyed the party for the most part, but as the evening wore on she found her energy begin to flag. Terry, though, ignored her excuses and dragged her off to dance to a particularly ambitious disco beat, and for a while she lost sight of Greg.

'Enough!' She sagged wearily against Terry. 'If I don't get some fresh air soon, I'm going to flake out!'

'Come along, Cinders,' Terry pulled her arm through his, 'let's away to find Prince Charming before you're turned back into a pumpkin!'

'What would I do without you, Buttons?'

But Greg was nowhere to be seen, so Terry gallantly abandoned Cindy/Candy and escorted Kate out through the French windows into the cool night air.

'Oh, this is better!' She breathed in appreciatively, clearing her foggy head of champagne. She had a feeling she had drunk a little more than she ought to have done. Her tolerance for alcohol was abysmally low. 'Wouldn't Dad love this garden? He always wanted a massive lawn. And those borders . . .'

She stopped dead. Terry, not paying that much attention, almost cannoned into her.

'Hold on, Kate. What's up?' He followed her mesmerised stare down the length of the garden. 'Oh, hell! Look, Kate, these things happen at parties. It's nothing . . .'

Kate did not hear him. She was thankful the closely entwined couple at the end of the garden were too engrossed in each other to notice her intrusion into what was a painfully obvious private moment.

Greg had his back turned to her, but there was no mistaking his tall, lithe figure. She could not make out the features of the face he was kissing, but the blonde hair spilling over his arm told its own story.

'I'd like to go back in now, please, Terry,' she whispered, unaware that her face was paper-white.

'Look, princess, I know it's probably already too late, but this is no time to lose your temper,' Terry urged as he hurriedly propelled her back into the noisy crowd. He pulled her roughly into his arms and began to sway her in time to the music, pressing her face into his chest to hide her features from any onlookers, and all the time he kept up with his urgent instructions. 'You know you'll hate yourself in the morning if you let yourself go. You have to face all these people at work, remember? Anyway, you wouldn't want to give that bitch the satisfaction of upsetting you, would you? Oh, bloody hell!' His grip tightened around her waist. 'Greg's on his way over here—and princess? I don't think you're the only one about to lose their rag! I think he's going to kill me if you don't let go! Princess? Kate? Oh—hi, Greg. You haven't seen Candy around anywhere, have you?'

'No. I was looking for a redhead, not a blonde.'

That did it!

Up until that moment Kate had been worried, for she had unfortunately recognised that she was not undergoing a mere loss of temper as Terry had justifiably supposed. For when her temper took her over, she felt nothing. Just before and just after, yes, but never during. And until Greg had spoken, Kate had been feeling too much. The wrong sort of feelings.

She should surely have felt happy, relieved at the very least, that Greg was turning his attention elsewhere. But she wasn't. All that consumed her was that those lips, which had been promised exclusively to her, were now playing their practised tune on someone else.

One promise, one measly little promise, of fidelity—and he couldn't even last out the engagement period!

Kate had waited for the anger to arrive, as it surely must, to blot out this curious sadness, and a pain which made her sick to her stomach. But now, like a passenger impatiently awaiting a late train, when the anger finally made a belated appearance, she welcomed it whole-heartedly.

Terry groaned aloud as she stiffly drew away from him.

'If you'll both excuse me, I'm going to get a drink of water.' A portion of Terry's lecture had managed to work its way through to her. It would be unpardonable of her to ruin the party, and she was fast approaching the stage when anything might happen.

It was only Terry's restraining hold which prevented Greg following her immediately.

'Look, Greg, I think I ought to warn you . . .'

'Warn me? Haven't you got that the wrong way round, Walsh?' Metallically glittering eyes focused dangerously on the hand holding him back. Unperturbed, Terry grinned, enjoying watching Greg in the grip of anger. He had been a little concerned at the lack of emotion Kate's fiancé had thus far displayed, but it seemed his fears were groundless. This was one angry man!

'And what do you imagine could happen in a room full of people, old man?' Terry looked pointedly around the room. The room was large, but so was the crowd, and although no one was paying any particular attention to them at the moment, the savagely polite expression on Greg's face did relax, until Terry added wickedly: 'Of course, had we been in a similar clinch in private—say, down the end of the garden, for example . . .'

Greg's composure did not falter for a moment, though Terry was astute enough to see through the mask as comprehension dawned. 'Good luck, Greg. You're sure going to need it!'

The first glass of water was barely sufficient to reduce Kate's rage by so much as a degree. So she poured another, sipping carefully this time, instead of gulping. The deserted kitchen was a haven, cool and uncluttered. Until Greg walked in.

'Terry tells me I owe you an apology,' he began warily, watching her closely.

'I thought we'd already agreed not to mouth words we didn't mean at each other,' Kate countered, 'eye of the storm' calmly.

'So we did.' He hesitated, his sharp gaze travelling over her white face. 'I'd be grateful if you could manage to hold on to your temper for a while, Kate.' He paused. Then, incredibly, 'I promised Caroline a lift home. Marchant has been drinking a little too freely.'

Kate watched with clinical detachment as Greg appeared to brace himself for whatever was to come. Of course, the last time she had felt like this she had slapped his face, so he was wise to expect trouble. Kate hated to disappoint people.

'I have a better idea, Greg. Why don't we dispose of it now, then we won't have to worry about it erupting in front of a third party?'

'I don't know what you have in mind, Kate, but . . .'

He shouldn't have grabbed her. He really shouldn't. At the

very least, he should have removed the couple of blonde hairs clinging so tenaciously to his shirt.

She did not hear his voice. She knew with utter clarity what she was about to do, and an earthquake would not have stopped her. She had known, of course, the moment he entered the kitchen. It could even have been the reason she poured herself a second glass of water.

She even knew what the consequences of such an action could be, and was sensible enough to be terrified at the thought.

But she still flung the contents of her glass in Greg's astonished face.

'I think I'll walk home—I seem to have a lot of energy to burn. Do thank Sam and Marie for the lovely party, won't you?'

She was a hundred yards down the road when the Mercedes caught up with her, as she had known all along it would. Her heart leapt wildly into her throat when she caught sight of his face. His features were contorted with rage as great as any she had ever felt, his lips drawn back against his teeth in a snarl. Kate could not have been more frightened had she suddenly come face to face with a rabid dog.

'Get in!' he ordered. Kate did as she was bid, still shaking from the after-effects of her own loss of control. His hands were gripping the steering wheel until his knuckles showed white, and Kate was in no doubt that he wished it was her neck he was throttling. No sooner had she fastened her seat-belt than he let in the clutch and the car roared away from the kerb.

'Caroline not with you, then?' Kate heard herself say with horror, amazed that she could sound so mockingly polite.

'Don't say another word, Kate!' he growled. 'Right now, I'm torn between giving you the beating of your life, and making love to you in the back seat of the car! And I haven't done that since I left my teens!'

'I'll take the beating, if you don't mind,' she whispered shakily, the words hardly audible even to herself, but Greg's acute hearing picked them up. His nostrils flared, a white line appearing around his tightly pursed lips, then he swerved the car up a rough-hewn path and stood on the brakes.

Kate loosened her seat-belt and grabbed for the door handle, intent on escape.

'The door's locked, Kate!' he taunted her, mercilessly yanking her around in his arms as if she were nothing more than a rag doll. Kate was unaware of the tears coursing down her cheeks, but the sight made Greg draw back from whatever he was about to do.

He let her go abruptly, sitting back and snapping on the interior light, and told her to do something about her face.

'I left my handbag behind,' she whispered, hating the quivering waver in her husky voice.

'Here.' He handed it to her. 'It seems Walsh knew what was in store. He threw it at me as I was leaving.'

Kate did what she could to repair the damage, but she was still a pitiful sight when she finished. Greg spared her one glance, encompassing her distress, and swore, quietly and with a fluency she could only applaud.

'I frightened you then, didn't I?' he asked without a trace of emotion.

'Yes.' What else could she say?

'Then perhaps you'll think twice next time?'

'Next time?' Her voice rose shrilly. 'You mean you intend to humiliate me like that again?'

He frowned darkly. 'Humiliate you? What are you talking about?'

'I'm talking about that passionate little clinch in the garden!'

He brought his fist down hard on the steering wheel in exasperation, breathing deeply before slanting a sideways glance at her. 'If you were looking that closely,' he bit out sarcastically, 'you would have seen the passion was all on Caroline's side.'

'Oh, fine! That makes it all hunky dory, I suppose. I didn't notice you fighting to defend your virtue!'

'That was not what motivated you to fling that glass in my face.' A dull flush appeared on his cheekbones.

'No,' Kate agreed blandly. 'I lost my temper—I did warn you about it, if you remember?' Her eyes hardened. 'Being treated with such a lack of respect tends to have that effect on me.'

Her words fell into a taut silence, until Greg restarted the engine.

'I didn't intend to humiliate you, Kate, no matter how it might have looked,' he told her quietly a few moments later. And, for some perverse reason of her own, Kate believed him. 'My—association with Caroline ended more than six months ago. Tonight was the first occasion we've met since then. She . . .' he paused, slanting her an assessing look, 'she wanted to say goodbye, and I thought it best to have some privacy. Obviously, I was mistaken. For that, and any embarrassment I may have inadvertently caused you, I apologise. But I warn you now, Kate,' he went on harshly. 'I will not tolerate a repeat performance of that little tantrum.'

'Just for the record, Greg, I will not tolerate any more goodbye scenes!' Her face was set in mutinous lines. His soft chuckle following hard on the heels of such frightening rage was disarming.

'One little kiss, Kate? It hardly constitutes a capital offence.'

'It does in my book,' she stated categorically.

Fortunately, they drew up outside her home at that moment. Greg laid a restraining hand on her arm as she made to leave the car.

'I shan't be seeing you until the ceremony.'

'Oh, what a shame!' Kate pouted with blatantly false disappointment. He laughed.

'I find myself looking forward to taming you, Kate. And I shall, if it's the last thing I do.'

'Oh, it will be, Greg,' she promised faithfully with poisonous sweetness. 'It will be!'

So, was it possible she had been in love with Greg all along? Or could it be some sort of sexual jealousy she had experienced? Did love arrive out of the blue, complete with fireworks and trumpets blaring? Or was it an emotion growing out of lesser, simpler feelings? Was it this gut-wrenching, painful intoxication she felt when Greg looked at her? Or was it the warm, comfortable glow shared by her parents?

Surely love brought with it warmth, not the chilling ice surrounding her heart? It would engender kindness, not the desire to inflict pain. It would make one happy, not cause this bitter misery and confusion.

No. Her logic assured her she could not be in love with Greg. She dared not be in love with him. This physical infatuation already put her too much in his control.

She had to stop thinking in terms of love. He did not know the meaning of the word. And even Kate would have bet that he would never allow her to teach him.

CHAPTER SEVEN

'WE'RE HERE!'

Kate sat up abruptly, surprised to find she had actually managed to doze off. She looked around her with interest.

'Here' was Sam and Marie's weekend bungalow over the border into Wales. Kate had adamantly refused to state a preference of honeymoon locations, much to Greg's displeasure. But Kate had shrugged eloquent shoulders at him and roundly declared that since his only interest was to get her into bed, the surrounding scenery was superfluous to requirements. She had noted the tightening of his lips with the same fatalistic air that had protected her through the past weeks, and the subject had been dropped.

But now she changed her mind. The bungalow was ensconced in a beautiful setting, allowing a panoramic view of the surrounding Welsh hills. Kate loved it on sight. It also boasted a huge secluded swimming pool which she noted with a lightening of spirit, a feeling which just as quickly vanished when she caught sight of Greg's determined face.

Kate found it impossible to hold that look. Her mind groped for some sort of defence mechanism to come to her aid, but she could summon nothing. Her anger, her defiance, appeared to have deserted her. Where was the point to resistance anyway? The deed was done. They were married and each would have to find a way to live together without tearing the other to pieces in the process.

She recognised that, knew it would be a self-defeating gesture to force them to live all the time on the edge of an argument. She could not live that way. It had been hard enough to cope with the disharmony her father had wrought in those few short weeks—the thought of her own marriage becoming a battlefield was distressing in the extreme.

But how to communicate such thoughts without feeling

she had surrendered totally to Greg's demands?

She was torn between wanting him to again become the teasing friend who had cared for her when she was sick, and needing him to remain the impersonal man she had married. At least, with the latter, she might be allowed some measure of resistance as a sop to her pride.

But right now, his dark mood was filling her with apprehension for the night to come. He was desperate enough to have married her, wasn't he? And she knew, with uncanny precision, that he resented her power to force him into such a situation. He might have deprived her of the freedom to choose, but hadn't she unwittingly done the same to him?

Mechanically, she prepared a light supper for them both. Someone had thoughtfully stocked the fridge with a quantity of cold meats and salad ingredients—also a bottle of champagne which Kate studiously ignored. Greg, however, opened it with a sardonic glance towards his new wife.

'Am I to take it you don't feel like celebrating?'

The insolently comprehensive gaze accompanying his mocking drawl brought a tinge of colour to her wan face.

They ate in complete and hostile silence, Kate merely playing with the food on her plate, although she downed more than her share of champagne. She was almost relieved when the meal was over and the bone-snapping tension of the last hour gave way to nervous resignation.

'I'm going to have a bath,' she declared shakily, and rose from the table. Greg looked up in surprise, then his brows lowered ominously at the sight of her strained face.

'Anne Boleyn on the way to meet the executioner's axe?' he taunted. 'I thought I'd probably have to carry you screaming and kicking to the bedroom.'

With a purposeful tread, he moved swiftly around the table, giving her no chance to retreat.

'There are two ways we can go about this, Kate,' he began warily, refusing her attempt to pull away from the hypnotic quality of his hard grey eyes. 'If you could try to relax, I'll do my best to make this as easy and pleasurable as possible for you. If you could give yourself to me . . .'

'Give myself to you?' she repeated in a shaking voice. 'When I give myself to a man it will be because I love him. Not because he's forced me . . .' She stopped, took a deep breath and met his iron features a shade more calmly. 'I don't know what you expect from me tonight, Greg. But whatever it is, you're going to have to take it. I have no doubts about your ability to force a response from me. And there's no point in getting angry with me . . .' she added with determination as his fingers bit cruelly into the soft flesh of her upper arms. 'You're the one who wanted an honest relationship between us. If you'd wanted someone to fall into your arms with delirious joy, you should have married one of your bloody alternatives!'

'Back to Caroline again, are we?' he sneered, letting her go as if her touch disgusted him. 'For your information, my loving *wife*,' his lips twisted on the word, 'Caroline Sterling would have danced naked on top of Big Ben if she thought she could get a ring out of me!'

'As I recall, a *loving* wife was the last thing you wanted,' Kate hit back, breathing hard.

'How right you are!' he agreed after a few moments' tense silence. 'Very well, Kate, you've made your point. Run away to your virginal bed. You're safe for tonight at least. I'm not in the mood for rape!'

Kate could hardly believe her ears. By the time she had assimilated the fact that he no longer intended to consummate their marriage there and then, he had disappeared. Overcome by an impulse she could not explain, she ran after him, finding him standing at the liquor cabinet in the lounge.

'Greg! I . . .' He turned as if he had been shot.

'Kate, I warn you now, it would take very little to change my mind!'

'But . . .' Her eyes widened in horror at the amount of whisky he had poured for himself. He raised the glass in a mockingly taunting salute before taking a hefty swallow.

'A man should be allowed a little pleasure on his wedding night, don't you think?' And he laughed. Kate simply did not know how to cope with this dark mood. He had withdrawn completely. So she stood helplessly staring in consternation as he drained the glass so quickly she winced for him.

'Go to bed, Kate. Now!'

She fled.

Surprisingly, sleep claimed her almost immediately, and for several hours her fatigued brain embraced the welcome relief from tension.

It was still dark when she awoke to the realisation that she had been a little too clever for her own good. The flannelette monstrosity of a nightgown she had filched from her mother's wardrobe might have been—in her father's words—a passion-killer, but it was hardly suitable attire for such a hot, muggy summer night. She was bathed in perspiration, the material of her virginal nightgown sticking uncomfortably to her skin. And she knew she would get no further sleep that night unless she cooled down.

She waited a moment to accustom herself to the darkness, before swinging her feet to the floor, only gradually becoming aware that she was no longer alone in the huge bed. Greg was sprawled on the other side, his arm flung across his eyes, his chest gleaming nakedly in the moonlight. He obviously had more sense than she.

Her heart missed a beat as she rose as silently as possible and padded along to the adjoining bathroom. She firmly closed her mind to all else but the relief of the cool spray on her overheated body as she stood revolving for several minutes under the shower.

She slowly towelled herself dry, looking with distaste at her discarded nightgown and knowing she could not bring herself to put it on again. Instead, she wrapped a towel sarong-wise around her body and peeped cautiously into the bedroom. There was no movement from the bed.

Heaving a silent sigh of relief, she made her way to the dressing-table, the moonlight helping her find a thinner covering. She hesitated beside the bed, debating whether or not she should go in search of somewhere else to spend the night, but practical common sense told her she was being silly. She could smell the whisky fumes from where she was standing. It did not take a genius to work out that Greg had probably drunk himself into a stupor. Besides, she did not have the energy to make up another bed.

She felt oddly guilty as she slid into the bed, taking care to keep on her own side. It was positively uncharacteristic for Greg to behave in such a manner—but then hadn't the last few weeks proved she knew precious little about the real Gregory Courtney? It was a disturbing thought on which to drift to sleep, but one shattered a few moments later when a heavy hand fell across her waist and jerked her to the middle of the bed.

'Greg . . .?'

'Yes, indeed,' a slurred disembodied voice enveloped her through the darkness.

Kate pushed vainly at him.

'No! Greg . . . you're drunk!'

'No, Kate.' Sure, sinfully practised hands quickly divested her of the nightgown she had only seconds before put on. 'I tried, I really did. But you're the only thing capable of intoxicating me.' His head dipped to the newly perspiring hollow between her breasts. 'You shouldn't have woken me, Kate.'

And all her protests were swallowed by his urgently seeking mouth.

Eighteen . . . nineteen . . . twenty.

Kate completed her last lap of the pool and pulled herself out of the water. She felt far more human after the violent exercise she had just subjected her body to.

This really was a beautiful place, she decided. The sun was hot on her back as she dangled her feet into the cooling water. Her earlier tour of inspection had revealed a total of three bedrooms and two bathrooms—one of which boasted the largest, most sybaritic sunken bath she had ever imagined. The kitchen was a dream. Sam and Marie certainly did themselves proud!

And all because of Greg, a little voice murmured in her ear. From the little Marie had let slip, she and Sam appeared to have had a lot more to do with Greg's upbringing than his own parents. And this was their reward.

Though Sam certainly earned every penny of his salary, Kate had to admit. Greg might provide the driving force behind the firm, but it was Sam's hard-slogging attitude to his job which put Greg's ideas into action. They complemented each other well.

Eventually, hunger drove her back into the bungalow. She had skipped breakfast, eager to get out and explore the views which beckoned her—and also eager to escape Greg. She had not seen him that morning. He had still been sleeping heavily when Kate left their bed.

'Good morning, Kate.' She jumped as Greg's quiet greeting reached her in the doorway to the dining area. To her amazement, he was putting a bowl of salad on the table, obviously prepared by himself. He looked quite unlike his usual former self. He was wearing an old, faded pair of jeans and a turquoise sweatshirt. Unfairly, there was no sign of his over-indulgence in the whisky bottle, except that his chin was darkened by stubble. Kate had never seen him unshaven. And he was looking at her.

She was glad she had thought to put on a thin yellow wraparound skirt over her swimsuit. It afforded her a little more composure under his intent scrutiny.

'I think it's more afternoon, really . . .' she offered inanely, and gestured towards the table. 'There was no need . . .'

'Did I hurt you, Kate?' Kate closed her eyes briefly. Trust Greg to come straight to the point! No leading gently into the subject, no beating around the bush. When she opened her eyes it was to surprise an expression of self-disgust on his face.

'I . . . No.' She licked dry lips, oddly anxious to dispel his stress. 'I mean—just a bit, but I suppose that was unavoidable.'

'Yes,' he agreed tightly, still holding himself stiffly. 'But I could have made it a little more—rewarding for you. It can't have been—pleasant, shall we say?' His brows rose in question.

Kate's face burned. Was it really necessary to have a post-mortem? She had spent all morning trying to avoid even thinking about what had happened, and now it seemed Greg wanted to recount events detail by disturbing detail.

'Well, as a matter of fact, it was! Pleasant, I mean,' she burst out, her embarrassment making her bluster. And she was not lying—not really, despite his look of disbelief. It had been pleasant—much more so, if she were to be totally honest. At least until he had rolled off her and fallen immediately into a deep sleep—the amount of whisky he had drunk finally catching up with him.

She had no intention of admitting to the ache of unsatisfied arousal which had left her wide awake for what remained of the night, or of the longing to participate fully in the magic of their first union. He had been so very gentle until that last stunning moment when his hoarse cry signalled a total loss of control.

'You're very forgiving, Kate,' he said quietly. Kate looked away in confusion. Surely it should have been easier to hate him this morning, but . . .

'Some things are easier to forgive than others. Besides, I've told you, it doesn't apply in this case. I—it was—nice, OK?' Her chin lifted defiantly, daring him to question her further.

'OK, Kate.' His hands spread wide in a gesture of acceptance. 'I know better than to question my good fortune in getting off so lightly!' He slanted her a crooked grin. 'Knowing your temper, I expected quite a lecture this morning!' There was still a question mark hanging in the air between them.

Kate chose to ignore it. 'I'm sure the thought had you shaking in your shoes.' She folded her arms across her chest, her generous mouth curving with a wry visitation of humour. Greg's brows rose, a bland expression replacing the tense wariness.

'Well, I seem to remember promising you dynamite. I wasn't sure a damp squib would be an adequate substitute.'

She tried to stop herself laughing, but it was no use. Greg looked so different when he smiled, his eyes crinkling at the corners, a warm silvery light in their depths and that annoyingly incongruous dimple flashing in one lean cheek.

'Ah well, perhaps it's as well I don't know the difference.'

'Not yet, anyway.'

Kate blushed anew at the sensual promise.

They passed the afternoon quite amicably. They discovered a mutual passion for cards and chess. Greg challenged her to several games, winning the first three with humiliating ease before Kate found her stride, but even then the best she could manage was a symbolic stalemate.

As evening approached, Greg announced that they would be eating out. Kate acquiesced immediately, hoping things would be easier with other people around. Greg was becoming dangerous in this affable mood. He had proved to her the night before that she had nothing to fear from him physically.

Even though she had not yet touched the heights of passion he had taught her she was capable of attaining, he had shown great consideration for her inexperienced state. No, physically, she knew it was only a matter of time before they were in perfect accord. Emotionally, it was another matter. Greg could keep the two separated. Kate simply did not know if she would be able to follow his example.

She took a quick bath and dressed in a simple white wraparound dress, leaving her hair free, for some unaccountable reason. Greg, to her relief, was dressed equally casually in brown shirt and trousers.

'Ready?' His eyes travelled over her impassively as he jangled the car keys in his pocket.

They ate at a small, intimate restaurant a few miles outside the town. The dance floor was so minute, Kate spared a moment to wonder why the proprietors had troubled to provide one. She was to discover the reason before the evening was over.

Greg put himself out to be charmingly attentive. So much so, she was beginning to notice curious glances being sent their way. When he pulled her suddenly resisting body on to the dance floor, all eyes were riveted upon them.

'Relax,' Greg ordered softly into her ear, holding her far too close for comfort.

'But everyone is staring at us!' she hissed back, knowing full well that a red stain of selfconsciousness was spreading over her face.

'Everyone likes to look at newlyweds, Kate,' he murmured as he nuzzled her earlobe. Kate knew she could not pull away from him without causing a scene.

'So that's why you brought me here,' she muttered angrily, ridiculously near to tears at the way she had been tricked. 'Because they all know you!'

'That's right,' he agreed, unabashed. She could sense his mocking smile, and seethed. Had she so wounded his pride the previous night by forcing him to take that he had determined that tonight she should give? As the evening drew on, she knew she had hit on the truth. Greg dragged her off to dance between each course of their meal. Whether or not he had bribed the small band, Kate would never know, but each time they rose from their table, the music slowed in tempo. By the end of the evening Kate was ready to scream in frustration.

Greg, true to form, took full advantage, moulding her closer and closer to the hard line of his body until he was practically making love to her on the dance floor, oblivious of their benign onlookers. At last, Kate could stand no more, and shakily told him she wanted to leave.

'So do I, Kate,' he murmured back, his voice lowly intimate, his lips curving in a sensuous echo of the message contained in his darkened eyes.

Horribly conscious of every sly glance in their direction, Kate straightened her back, lifted her chin and preceded him from the restaurant.

Back at the bungalow, she declared tersely that she was going to take a shower. Without sparing a glance for her husband, she practically ran to the bathroom, pausing only to pick up her dressing-gown. She wrapped a towel around her hair and stepped into the shower with a desperate hope that the stinging needles of tepid water would counteract the sensations Greg had aroused. It was criminal that he could affect her so—basically when she knew he was manipulating her time and time again. And every time she was only too willing to believe the best—as today, when she thought he was attempting to become a friend when he was simply paving the way to becoming her lover.

A light hand descending on her shoulder caused her to scream with fright, even more so when she caught the kindling fire of Greg's hot glance as his eyes travelled the length of her wet, naked body. She stood in paralysed turbulence as he calmly picked up a tablet of soap and lathered his hands.

Then she felt those soapy hands sliding over her breasts. 'No!' Her hoarse cry sounded feeble in the confined space of the shower cubicle. Every way she turned brought her up against his long, lean, unashamedly aroused body. His hands reached around her neck and moved with a featherlike caress down each knuckle of her spine. She had never known anything so erotic as the brush of his wet nakedness against her own, and the desire to resist—even the reasons why she must resist—deserted her, leaving her defenceless, unprotected against the onslaught of an expert sensualist.

She stood mesmerised as Greg towelled her dry, smoothing the soft towel over every inch of her trembling body. Then, shockingly, she realised he was no longer using the towel. The lightly rough friction against her skin was his tongue, stroking, tasting, drinking in her sweetness. Sensing that her legs would no longer support her, Greg lifted her high into his arms and carried her with effortless ease to the king-sized bed.

He drew a rasping breath as he was at last able to survey her naked form. Kate was unable to do anything but lie breathtakingly supine as his eyes drank their fill of her. From her tumbling waves splayed over the pillow, over her mesmerised face—wide slumbrous eyes and softly quivering mouth. Down the long column of her throat, lingering on the fast-beating pulse at the base. Over gently rounded shoulders to her breasts, nipples hardening in instinctive betrayal as his gaze caressed them. Down over the slender, jutting curve of her hipbone, around the flatness of her stomach, to the dark plateau beneath. Down the length of long, shapely limbs, even to the curling toes on small feet.

And Kate could not move. Pinned to the bed by that penetrating surveillance, she felt as if he had already made love to her. The shock deepened as their glances collided.

Greg's face was flushed, his jaw clenched rigid with white-hot desire. When could she ever have thought him cold-blooded? She watched in ever-increasing fascination as he slowly removed his towel to reveal his own impressive physique. Hard muscles, hair-roughened chest, lean hips, long, loose limbs. It had been too dark to see him the previous night, but now his sheer masculine beauty took her breath away.

She should be fighting him, she knew that. In the back of her mind warning bells were ringing raucously, but not loudly enough to force her limbs to obey her half-hearted order to resist.

Piercing pleasure shot through her as he bent low and took the hardened tip of her breast deep into his mouth, his hands effortlessly pinning her arms above her head to grant him easier access.

'Dear heaven! Please, Greg . . . you must . . .' Her protest—if it was indeed a protest—was lost as his lips covered hers and his hand moved to discover the curve of her hipbone—every new caress causing her to arch into him.

'It's good, Kate. Better than I could have imagined.' His silvery gaze captured her wide green eyes, reading clearly the mirrors of her arousal.

He continued to kiss and caress every inch as her hands finally surrendered and made their own journeys of discovery across his chest and back, her own pleasure growing as she felt him tremble beneath her hands as they moved across the flatness of his stomach and lower—until Greg's shaking hand stayed hers.

'Not yet, Kate,' he murmured raggedly against her lips.

She drew back slightly at the last moment, mindful of a remembered brief shaft of pain, but Greg sensed her fear and patiently calmed her once more with his lips and hands—stroking her to a state of mindless frenzy.

He moved slowly within her, giving her time to adjust to the alien though instinctive rhythm. His breath grew hot on her face as passion quickened his pace, overtaking the rigid control he had up until now maintained. His mouth plundered hers, scorching her lips with white-hot flames of desire until their crescendent cries echoed through the stillness of the night.

Kate lay absolutely still, stunned by the violent emotions still raging through her. The heat of Greg's body on hers lingered in a faint film of perspiration. Slowly she turned her head to the side, dreading the glow of triumph she expected to be etched on his hard features. She was wrong. He looked as thoroughly shaken as she still felt.

'Well,' he said finally, breathlessly. 'Does that come under the heading of "nice" too?' he mocked her gently, the silver light in his eyes shining down on her still roused features. 'Stop fighting it, Kate. Don't you know your body will betray you every time from now on?' To emphasise his assertion, his hand made a casual sweep up her thighs, over her stomach, to rest on the undercurve of her breast. He laughed softly as she shuddered, bitterly aware of his naked proximity. How could she ever resist him again now she knew the full glory of the dynamite he had promised her? She hoped with all her heart she would find a way.

'It's good between us, Kate. Can't you feel that?' His voice was husky, his eyes again kindling with the light of renewed desire. 'Be thankful we're one of the few couples to achieve such perfect pleasure.' His eyes ran over her flushed nakedness. 'It's pretty rare, believe me.'

'You knew it would be like this?' she whispered incredulously, her eyes widening in disbelief. Greg gave a short bark of laughter.

'If I had the least idea, Kate, then nothing on earth would have made me wait this long for you.' His head lowered to pull the tip of her breast between his teeth again in an erotic sucking motion. 'I want you again, Kate. Now!'

'Go to hell!' she muttered fiercely as her body responded blindly to his call.

'Oh, no, Kate.' His white teeth were bared in a grin of genuine masculine amusement. 'I'm going to heaven. And you're coming with me!'

And she did. Shamelessly.

CHAPTER EIGHT

'PRINCESS? Why on earth didn't you get the shop to do the alterations on those curtains?' Terry asked plaintively as Kate jabbed her finger with the sewing needle for the hundredth time.

Marie Goodis and Alissa McNaught exchanged a look which translated loosely as an exasperated 'Men!' and bent their heads back to sewing hems.

Kate sucked at the small puncture wound, regarding Terry balefully. It was just as well he hadn't witnessed the earlier fiasco when she had sewn the material on her lap to her jeans!

'Because they wanted to charge ten pounds a pair for alterations. Daylight robbery after the amount I spent!' Kate's voice rang with the indignation she still felt.

But Terry obviously did not see the sense of her argument, despite the older women's approving nods.

'If you're so pennypinching, how come you're giving a perfectly good bed to the Salvation Army and replacing it with one practically the same?' he pointed out with perfect masculine logic. It was also a subject Kate had no wish to pursue, not with Marie's eyes resting thoughtfully on her downbent head.

'I'm changing all the furniture in the bedroom, Terry. The old headboard didn't match the colour scheme.' When she was certain her own colour had subsided, she lifted her head. 'A question of aesthetics,' she added with an 'I don't expect a mere male to understand' air.

He didn't.

'Typical! Put a woman's name on your credit card and you may as well sign a pact with the devil! What did Greg have to say about it all?'

Kate swallowed on the lump of pure guilt which settled in her throat. 'Well—er—nothing really.'

Terry remained unconvinced. Marie and Alissa exchanged another telling look.

'Have you finished that curtain rail yet?'

'Nag, nag, nag! No, I haven't. I'm taking a well-earned tea break. Unless you've any cold beer handy?' His eyes brightened with hope.

Kate took pity on him. It really was rather nice of him to give up his Saturday to help her redecorate the master bedroom. The four of them had done so well, only the finishing touches were now required. Kate had been working like a beaver to get everything finished by the time Greg returned from Scotland.

'I seem to remember picking up a six-pack yesterday.'

Terry headed for the kitchen.

'So Greg has no idea you're decorating, then, Kate?' asked Marie, hazel eyes innocently interrogative.

'We—ell . . .'

'Oh, Katherine, do you think that's wise? Gregory doesn't seem the type to take kindly to surprises.'

'Nonsense, Alissa! Best tactics, if you ask me!' Marie nodded decisively. 'It's tears with Sam. That man can't bear to see me cry! Turns into a complete jellyfish. He'll agree to anything.'

Alissa looked a little shamefaced as she confessed her method. 'The dripping tap technique—it works like a dream. Of course, I have to plan well in advance.'

Marie looked interested. 'Mmm—I don't think it would work with Sam. He wouldn't notice a hint if it jumped up and smacked him in the face! No, Kate, I think you're handling this right.' Kate, who had not been consciously handling anything, managed to look suitably thankful for the pearls of wisdom. 'Yes, it would have to be the direct approach with Greg,' Marie added musingly.

'Direct? Directly behind his back, you mean!' Terry laughed uproariously, almost choking on his beer as the three women jumped guiltily at the sound of his voice.

'I tell you, if ever I'm foolish enough to get married, I'm keeping my wife well away from you three!'

'She won't need us, Terence,' Alissa declared. 'Any

woman crafty enough to get you to the altar . . .'

'Enough!' Terry threw up his hands in surrender. 'I'm going to finish the curtain rail. I know my place in your scheme of things.'

'Oh, dear!' Kate bit her lip. 'Do you think perhaps . . .?'

'Too late to get cold feet now, my dear!' Marie giggled at her consternation. 'There! I do believe we've finished!' She tied off the cotton and sat back, satisfaction in every line of her. 'That wasn't so bad, was it?'

'Wasn't it?' Kate looked pointedly at her needle-marked fingers. 'Personally I think it may have been worth the ten pounds after all.'

'Where's the ironing board, Katherine?'

'Oh—in one of the kitchen cupboards, I think.'

'You think?'

'Don't look at me like that, Mom!' Kate grew defensive. 'Mrs Arthur does her nut if I do the washing up. I think ironing carries the death penalty!'

'Oh, she's wonderful, though, isn't she, Kate? She's looked after Greg since he moved here,' Marie explained for Alissa's benefit. 'I think even Greg's a little in awe of her.'

Kate's answering snort was eloquence itself. 'Well, I do think he could have warned me,' she protested, remembering her first interview with the frighteningly efficient daily woman.

The one thing Kate and Greg had agreed on was to cut Kate's working week in half. Her duties were now shared between herself and Susan Henshaw, and another girl had been drafted into the office to make up the shortfall. Kate still handled the majority of the work, though, since she helped Greg in the evenings.

So, with a couple of days a week to herself, it was only natural to assume Mrs Arthur would not be required to work as many hours. In fact, Kate would have been just as happy to dispense with her services altogether. But the woman had different ideas. Somehow, during the course of the interview, Kate found herself agreeing to increase the woman's hours rather than reduce them, sadly deducing that she lacked the killer instinct necessary on occasions with employees. Greg had thought it hilarious.

But at least she was now able to put her free hours to good use. Retaining her position bolstered her independent streak, but now she had a little time free from Greg's ever-disturbing presence.

'This sudden decision to redecorate wouldn't have anything to do with the clanger I dropped the other evening, would it?' asked Marie as soon as they were alone.

'Clanger?' Kate asked blankly, more to gain time than for the answer she already knew.

'Mmm. You remember—about Caroline Sterling being responsible for the interior design of this place?'

Kate sighed. Marie had become too good a friend in some respects over the past month. She was grateful for the older woman's basic common sense. She also wished Marie was not quite so astute. Prevarication was not going to do Kate any good with those sharp hazel eyes fixed on her.

'Well, it might just have tipped the scales.' Kate stretched the truth as far as she felt able.

'You don't have anything to fear from that woman, Kate. If Greg had been half-way serious about her, then believe me, I would have known about it,' Marie stated firmly.

Kate believed her.

Marie and Sam had been fairly frequent and always welcome visitors over the six weeks she and Greg had been married. Kate looked forward to their visits. They brought out a side of Greg Kate would have liked to know a lot better than she was allowed.

And it *had* been an innocent remark by Marie that had caused the last three days' frantic activity. Kate had complained mildly that however many little changes she made around the apartment, she could not truthfully feel at home there.

Marie had nodded sagely, understanding Kate's dilemma immediately. 'You have to realise it was basically designed as a bachelor apartment. Trust that Sterling woman to specialise in such an area!'

Kate had gone very still as Marie clapped a hand over her mouth in dismay, and looked towards Greg for an explanation he seemed only too happy to provide.

'Caroline's a partner in a firm of interior designers. She—er—looks after this side of the business.' And his eyes had dared her to make what she wanted of that. Had they been alone, her reaction might well have been more volatile. But, conscious of her friend's discomfort, she had merely murmured reflectively,

'I always knew there'd be a logical reason why I hate this place!'

And she had decided there and then to stamp the apartment with her own signature. It had seemed provident that Greg was called away to Scotland the next day to solve a dispute over manning levels. Kate had wasted no time. The first thing to be thrown out was the bed!

She had stared at it with loathing the night before, images of Greg and Caroline nakedly entwined upon it refusing to leave her in peace, and giving her the impetus to resist Greg with a little more conviction than had thus far been the case.

Not that resistance was much use. Greg knew full well that she was his the moment he touched her. Even a look was sometimes sufficient for the barriers to begin to crumble. But at least Kate had the satisfaction of knowing those barriers afforded her husband a great measure of annoyance.

Kate enjoyed annoying Greg. Not a very nice trait in an otherwise very nice person, but one she was finding oddly exhilarating.

Adjusting to marriage had, by no stretch of the imagination been the nightmare she had envisaged. Mainly because Greg continued to treat her as if nothing had changed between them, during daylight hours, at least. But even the long summer evenings brought very little hint that he regarded her as anything more than his assistant. He brought masses of work home with him, and Kate was expected to help. She was even paid overtime!

It took a couple of weeks of this for her to understand that Greg had no intention of making their marriage a real one. The sexual side apart, he did not want a wife—did not want Kate to think of herself as a wife. And he did everything possible to keep an emotional distance between them.

'Don't get too caught up in the wifely gestures, Kate! I have no use for them!' he had declared harshly one morning when she automatically straightened his crooked tie—something she had done for her father and brothers more often than she could remember.

The words had hurt, and Kate had not learnt the trick of hiding her feelings from him. But however upset she was, she never allowed such cruelty to pass.

'Gaining a wife is one of the unfortunate consequences of getting married, Greg,' she told him calmly. 'You've always struck me as the type who willingly pays the price of his actions. Well, I'm it!'

The small changes she had made around the apartment could have been the cause of a lot more dissension had she not been prepared for his reaction. Indeed, she welcomed it. Any opportunity to punch holes in that unemotional persona, every tightening of his lips, every irritated lowering of his brows brought Kate a little glow of satisfaction. For she knew she was getting to him, burrowing under his skin, insinuating herself into all aspects of his life. And he did not like it one little bit.

He wanted her to change into one of the sophisticated types who presented no danger to him, was trying to coat her with the same shell of brittle cynicism with which he viewed relationships. Kate refused to fit the mould.

She rebelled in her own quiet way, calmly asserting herself when necessary, and otherwise going her own sweet, warmly spontaneous way.

But this, Kate had to admit, looking around her at the vast changes she had wrought in the master bedroom, might have been over the top. It was one of the few times she had let her temper get the better of her.

And your jealousy, she ruthlessly reminded herself. For, even though she implicitly believed Greg's explanation of that—association, any mention of Caroline Sterling still touched a raw spot. It was one thing to know one's husband was experienced. It was quite another to come face to face with one of those experiences!

And it was also one of the unpalatable facts which were

adding up to something Kate had tried hard to avoid, but was fast becoming inevitable. The more insight she gained into Greg's past, the more she understood what motivated him. And the more she understood him, the more she cared for him. Cared deeply. Even now she dared put her feelings no higher than that. Not until he too confessed that he cared for her—as a person, not just as a warm body to bury himself in at the end of the day.

And however distant and impersonal he was during the day, at night he made love to her with such unselfishness, such consideration, such burning intensity, that Kate was able to hope that he subconsciously, at least, felt something far more significant for her than the liking and respect he had already admitted.

She was sorely tempted to question Marie further about Greg's parents, knowing that his attitude towards marriage had been coloured, perhaps irrevocably, by their example. One thing Marie had inadvertently let slip was that Greg's mother had walked out on his father after the pit accident. Small wonder Greg was cynical! But Kate valiantly held her curiosity at bay, clinging a little superstitiously to the hope that Greg would one day trust her enough to tell her himself.

Meanwhile, though, Terry's call that he had completed his set task recalled her to the present day. She had curtains to hang!

'There! What do you think?' Kate did not trouble to hide her satisfaction at a job well done. The curtains glided open and shut with one little tug on the cord she was holding.

'It's beautiful, Kate! Really beautiful!' Marie declared with whole-hearted approval. 'I can't wait to see Greg's face!'

Kate's glow took a down-turn. 'I can!' she muttered morosely.

'Mm, a good strong cup of tea, I think.' her mother prescribed. 'Good for the nerves!'

'I'll come and help you, Alissa. Cheer up, Kate—they abolished hanging ages ago!' With which cheery message Marie followed Alissa into the kitchen.

Terry looked at Kate in comic consternation. 'Did that

mean what I think it means?'

'Mmm?'

'You haven't told Greg about any of this, have you?'

'We—ell, no,' she finally admitted with what she hoped was a winning smile.

It wasn't. Terry glared at her.

'I thought you were my friend!'

'I am . . . Look, love . . .'

'Don't you "love" me!' He began to gather his tools hastily together. 'I'm getting out of here before your old man turns up!'

Kate laughed. 'He's not due back until tomorrow!'

'I don't care! I'm going.' He started throwing spanners, screwdrivers and drilling bits into his tool kit. 'And you, my lady, will not breathe one word about my involvement in this. Understand?' He fastened the tool kit and strode from the room. 'I get enough funny looks from him as it is. If he found out I'd spent the whole day here . . .'

Kate, following hard on his heels—still giggling helplessly at his panic—stopped short at the sight which had Terry standing as stiff as a statue.

They exchanged patently guilty looks before turning back to face their fate.

'Look, old chap. I can explain . . .'

'You're not due back until tomorrow!'

Greg did not say a word. He stood stock still, looking at them, only hard eyes moving in a face which could otherwise be made of stone.

Kate groaned inwardly at that look. Back to square one, was the depressing thought as Greg took in her dishevelled appearance. She had tied her hair back that morning but knew precious little of it remained restrained. And her cheeks were undoubtedly the same colour as her dratted waves. She was also wearing her most disreputable pair of jeans, which did not help matters.

Once, just once, she would love to have the upper hand. It wasn't that much to ask, surely? But that day looked to be in the far distant future. It was certainly not today!

He, naturally, was his own impeccable self—dark grey suit,

discreet tie, pristine white shirt. And how he managed to look that way after a train journey from Scotland, Kate would never know.

Miraculously—or it seemed to Kate—Alissa and Marie chose that moment to bustle into the lounge with a laden tray.

'Gregory! You're home early! How nice,' Alissa beamed—then remembered what she had been up to and the smile faltered.

Marie simply said, 'Oh, dear,' and sat down.

Then someone knocked heavily on the door. 'I'll get it!' Kate very nearly ran straight past Greg, but was caught at the last moment by a heavy arm reaching around her waist and jerking her off her feet into much too close contact with her husband.

'Alissa? Would you mind answering the door, please?' Greg asked politely, before slanting a mildly enquiring look down at his wife's miserably resigned face. 'Your daughter has a few things to explain to me. Don't you, Kate?'

At least he didn't seem so angry any more, Kate saw as she peeped at him from under her lashes, and she felt a little courage seep back into her. She had only meant to annoy him a little bit, but once she had thrown out the bed, everything else seemed to snowball on her, until nothing remained of the original design in the bedroom. She had expected a certain amount of anger, but certainly not the rage she had felt hitting her in waves as he looked at her and Terry.

And anyway, why should he be angry before he's even discovered what I've done? Her brows drew together in a frown as she pondered on that question, but her mother had meanwhile opened the door.

'Er—Katherine? It's the man from the Salvation Army.'

'Oh, lord!' Greg's iron grip tightened even further. Kate bit her lip again, and tried to prise his fingers loose. 'This is turning into a French farce!' she muttered in despair, and gave up the idea of getting away. She turned her head in Terry's direction, absently noting the way that Marie was sitting drinking her tea with every sign of enjoyment. 'Terry? Would you help the man with the—um—' a glance at Greg's face did nothing to help her vocal cords work properly, '. . . bed, please?' she managed to croak.

'Right!' Terry, released at last from his frozen state, attempted a facsimile of his normal friendly grin. 'I'll—er—do that.'

Alissa inched her way around Greg's back, doing her best to stay out of his range of vision, and sat beside Marie. They all watched in silence as Terry and the man from the Salvation Army carried the bed from where it had been stored in the spare bedroom out of the apartment.

Kate, still imprisoned in Greg's hold, turned and addressed the knot in his tie.

'Would you—er—like some tea? It's fresh.'

'No. What I would like . . .' he stopped, his lips thinning as Terry sauntered back in. 'What I would like is the reason the four of you . . .' apparently he noticed at that moment Marie's quietly obvious enjoyment of the proceedings, and corrected himself '. . . the three of you look so guilty.'

A strangled sort of groan made its way out of Kate's mouth as Marie stood and declared it was time she and Alissa were on their way home. 'Our menfolk will be wondering where we've got to.' She divided the beam of her smile equally between them, and looked pointedly at Terry.

'Ah, yes. Right! I'll—er—give you both a lift, shall I?'

'Why, thank you, Terence,' Alissa accepted. 'See you soon, I hope, Gregory. I'm so sorry we have to dash off like this.'

They were gone before Kate could form words of protest, but their indecently hasty departure lit a spark of defiance in her.

'Miserable cowards!' she muttered as Greg at last allowed her feet to touch the ground. His hands moved absently up and down her spine, setting up a small spate of electric shocks throughout her system.

'You appear to have been abandoned to your fate, my lovely wife. Do I get that explanation now?'

Kate rested her head against his chest for a moment, savouring the feel of his arms around her. Such moments were rare, hugs and caresses were not part of their normal daily life.

'I think it would be easier to show you,' she said flatly, forcing herself to move away. She took his hand, not noticing his instinctive withdrawal amidst the rest of the turmoil chasing around her brain, and led him to the bedroom.

It was a long time before he spoke. Rather than try to read his expression, Kate followed his glance around the room.

The coldly stark white walls were now a warmer beige with deepening shades of brown highlighting the surrounds. The thick shagpile carpet was now a deep mahogany instead of pure white—a ridiculous colour for a carpet, Kate had always thought. The curtains she had sewn so diligently and resentfully that morning, and the new duvet cover, were a mass of swirling shades of green. The flimsy ultra-modern furniture had also been replaced by much more substantial shining mahogany. It gave, Kate thought, a more homey feel to the place.

'You don't like it, do you?' Her face fell at Greg's tightly controlled expression. 'Well, that's too bad! I have to live here too. And I can't stand . . .' Her voice trailed off as Greg started to pull the cord which closed the curtains.

'You did all this yourself?'

She gave a jerky nod. 'Well, Mom helped with the actual decorating. Marie and Terry came today to help finish off.'

'Mmm. It's very—you, somehow,' he said quietly, his gaze roaming her tense figure. 'Warm, solid—permanent. There's just one thing missing.'

'I——What's that?' she whispered, hardly daring to believe that he understood and accepted the message she had attempted to convey in the way she had decorated their room. Her breath stilled when he smiled at her and held out a compelling hand.

'Why, the christening of the bed, of course!'

Kate was surprised the next morning around noon by Terry dropping in unannounced.

'What are you doing here? Shouldn't you be propping up a bar somewhere?'

The timeless ritual of Sunday lunchtime had been reinstated now that her father was working again, and that should have meant Terry and Callum indulging in one hour's steady drinking, followed by her mother's famous roast beef and Yorkshire pudding.

Terry scowled at her.

'Yes, I should. I—er—left my tool kit behind.' He gave a furtive glance around the room. 'Where is he?' he mouthed.

'He's gone to see Sam.' Kate glanced at her watch. 'Actually, he should have been back before now.'

It took Kate little time to discover the real reason behind Terry's unexpected visit.

'What do you mean—you wanted to check everything was OK?' she asked after settling him down with one of the cans of beer left from the previous day.

'Well, I thought there might have been repercussions . . .' He lifted an ironic brow at Kate's self-conscious blush, and grinned. 'Mmm, so you've tamed him after all, eh?'

'Huh! That'll be the day!' Kate declared with a little more vehemence than Terry's joking tone warranted. She felt strangely jumpy today, maybe because of Greg's unpredictable reaction to her attempt to annoy him. He had not raised the subject again—even when she deliberately intimated that the lounge was the next item on her agenda. Was he at last beginning to accept her as his wife?

'You are happy with Greg, aren't you, princess?' Terry asked, concerned at her uncharacteristic cynicism.

'I don't think . . .'

'OK, OK!' he held up his hands. 'I know it's none of **my** business. But I have to say, I was a bit concerned when you first announced your marriage plans. He just didn't seem to be your type.' He smiled a little self-consciously. 'I mean, I know you would never marry for anything other than love—but I kind of got the impression . . . princess?'

When Kate first realised the track Terry's questions were taking, she had schooled her features to show nothing of the remaining bitterness she felt at Greg's manipulation of circumstances. But Terry's words struck a deep chord and she was struck by a lightning bolt of sure instinctive knowledge.

Greg would never have used that contract she had signed

against her family. Oh, he might have used it to force her to serve the stated two years as his assistant, but he would certainly never punish her family for something she had done. It simply was not his way of doing business. Why had she not seen that before?

It was as if she wanted an excuse to surrender to him . . . Oh, no! It surely could not be . . .?

'Princess?'

'I . . . Oh, excuse me!' she mumbled thankfully as the telephone rang. She jumped up with alacrity to answer it, steadying herself at the sound of the cool disembodied voice at the other end of the line.

'Am I speaking to Mrs Courtney?'

'Yes . . . Who . . .?'

'Alexandria Hospital here, Mrs Courtney. Your husband has been involved in an accident. It's not serious,' was the hasty assurance, 'but he did ask that I contact you to allay any worry about his late arrival home.'

'I'll be right there.'

'Oh, he did say not to . . .'

Kate did not hear any more. She replaced the receiver with a shaking hand and turned, white-faced, back to Terry.

'Greg's been involved in an accident. I have to go to the hospital.'

'I'll take you.'

'There's no need . . .'

'Princess, you're shaking like a leaf! I doubt you could even open the car door, let alone drive.'

The gentle caring in his voice was Kate's undoing. The tears, once started, could not be stopped.

'It's all right, baby. Ssh! He'll be OK. He's tough as old boots, is Greg.' Tenderly he rocked her limp body against his chest, crooning words of comfort in her ear, until some colour returned to her wan face. 'You love him an awful lot, don't you?'

'Do birds fly?' Her lips twisted in weary mockery. 'Incredible, isn't it? All this time and I never knew . . .'

'Princess?' Terry touched a hand to her wet cheek, brushing away her tears. 'I don't understand . . .?'

'It's a long story, Terry.' Finally Kate managed to pull herself together and searched for her handbag and jacket. 'One I don't really understand myself.'

All the warring emotions she had ever felt towards her enigma of a husband had crystallised at the sound of that briskly impersonal voice on the telephone.

So she was now completely defenceless. She was fathoms deep in love with Greg—had probably been in love with him from the very beginning. All those stupid lectures she had given herself had been a waste of time. Analysing something as basic as love, for heaven's sake! And all along she must have been aware, as Terry had said, that she could marry for no other reason than love. What other reason could there be?

She gave Terry a few details of her marriage on the way to the hospital. Her raw emotional state needed an outlet before she saw Greg. She was just as likely to fling herself into his arms declaring her love for all the world to hear—and she could imagine his reaction to that! But even knowing Terry was probably the safest person she could confide in, she drew a veil over most of it.

'You're wrong, Kate,' Terry told her firmly. 'Greg does care—enough to be insanely jealous of me, anyway.'

'What?' Her astonishment was most unflattering, as his wounded look told her.

'What do you imagine he thought yesterday, seeing us coming out of your bedroom—and looking guilty as hell?'

That gave her pause for thought. She had thought it strange that he should be so angry before he had discovered how she had disobeyed his instructions to leave the apartment alone. But to think that she and Terry . . .! The idea was ludicrous. It would be almost incestuous to think of Terry as her lover.

'Well, we could always put it to the test,' Terry offered—bravely, when one remembered his panic the previous day.

'No, Terry.' Kate remained unconvinced. 'I may not know the best way to reach Greg, but I'm certain that isn't it.' She pondered a moment. 'I think the only way to play this is straight.'

'Ah,' he nodded thoughtfully, then threw her a laconically amused grin. 'The direct approach behind his back! I get it.'

Kate laughed, grateful for his unflagging support, then she sobered, analysing what he had said.

'The direct approach behind his back'—hadn't that been what she had been doing since their return from honeymoon?

Kate knew now that it was. She had pretended she enjoyed annoying him, when really all she wanted was a reaction. Even a plate-throwing stand-up fight would have been preferable to the lowering of his brows and the stoic silence he was so good at maintaining. Normally Kate would have gone to great lengths to ensure a peaceful existence.

What was more, she realised with a lightening of her spirits, yesterday's fiasco had reaped results. Yesterday was the first time Greg had made love to her during the day since their honeymoon—long, beautiful, urgent love. And he had held her afterwards . . . not for long, admittedly, but it was more than before . . . Or was it merely the result of three days' abstinence?

'Wake up, Kate. We're here!'

Terry tracked Greg down to a curtained-off cubicle in the casualty department. Kate's heart nearly stopped beating at the sight of an incredibly fit-looking Greg calmly buttoning up his shirt as he sat glowering at them from the treatment couch.

'You're all right!' Kate accused him, ridiculously angry after the initial spurt of overwhelming relief. Greg gave a sardonic smile on noticing Terry fade discreetly away.

'As you see. Sorry if that upsets you.'

If possible, Kate went even paler than when she had first heard the news of his accident. She had just discovered she loved this man with the cold dispassionate eyes, and the thin lips which could wreak havoc on her senses even as he uttered such callous remarks.

She bit her lip hard in an effort to stop the flow of further tears, though her earlier breakdown was still very much in evidence, as Greg had just noticed. He muttered angrily, raking his fingers through his already dishevelled hair.

'I'm sorry, Kate, that was unnecessary.'

'Since when has that ever stopped you?' she returned bitterly, unable to conceal the hurt in her wide green eyes.

'Now, now, princess. No upsetting the hero of the hour!' Kate swirled around as Terry re-entered the cubicle.

'Shut up, Terry!' Greg ordered angrily.

'What do you mean?' Kate asked at the same time. Terry glanced at Greg, drawing enjoyment from his new partner's discomfort.

'I've just been regaled with your husband's exploits by a wide-eyed nurse out there. I do believe you've got them all in a dither, Greg.'

Kate stamped her foot in frustration. 'Will someone please tell me what's going on?'

'Nothing for you to concern yourself with,' Greg told her coldly.

'I see.' The colour flooded back into her face, showing up the angrily hurt sparkle in her eyes. 'Then as you're so obviously fit and well, I'll leave you to Terry's ministrations. I'll go home and put the insurance policies away!'

Greg's shout of laughter hit her as she pulled the curtain shut and stumbled headlong into the path of a burly middle-aged policeman.

'Ah, you wouldn't, by any chance, be Mrs Courtney, would you?' he asked after assuring himself that she had come to no harm.

'Yes——What . . .?'

The policeman handed her the keys to the Mercedes. 'I locked it up for him just as he asked. It's in a side street, just off the Solihull bypass. Oh, and if you could tell him the old lady's all right—a bit of shaken, of course, but . . .'

'Old lady?' Kate repeated parrot-fashion.

'Ah,' the policeman nodded understandably. 'One of our more modest heroes, eh?'

Kate blinked. 'I assumed he was involved in an accident?'

'Incident, more like, miss. Could have been very nasty too, without your husband lending a hand, that is. He saw a mob of youths harassing an old lady. They grabbed her handbag, but your husband gave chase. Only one of the mob pulled a knife on him. That's when he twisted his knee—turned a bit too sharpish, like. But he got the bag back—and two of those young yobbos,' he finished with evident satisfaction. 'If you'll tell him we'll be in touch if we need him in court, then.'

'Yes, of course.' Kate summoned a shakily polite smile. 'Thank you.'

CHAPTER NINE

WAS THERE any better way to make a man fall in love than to yell at him like a fishwife? Kate asked herself the question repeatedly as she went in search of a wheelchair to transport Greg to the car. The moment the policeman had mentioned Greg's injury, she was forced to recall the beads of sweat standing out on his forehead, the lines of strain around his mouth. Her anger dissolved completely at the thought of Greg—in pain.

He glared with disgust at the wheelchair she pushed into the cubicle five minutes later, but sank wearily into it without voicing a protest.

'Terry, can you drop me off at Greg's car?'

'Sure. That's what I'm here for. Kate was in no fit state to drive when she got the call.'

Greg held Terry's direct stare without a trace of emotion. 'Thank you,' he acknowledged eventually, and Kate hurriedly gave him the policeman's message. 'Remind me to get the woman's address. I'll send her some flowers or something.'

Kate met his hard challenging look with a sweet smile. 'It's already taken care of,' she assured him.

Getting Greg into Terry's car was a painful procedure Kate refused point-blank to repeat when Terry drew up behind the abandoned Mercedes. Greg's very failure to protest was enough to tell her he was in pain. She knew he disliked having to ask favours even of such a good friend as Sam. Kate had no hesitation.

She followed Terry's car at a more sedate pace, grateful for the opportunity to gather her wits in blessed solitude.

Greg's ability to hurt her seemed to have increased a hundredfold with her newly discovered vulnerability to him. Was she going to have to stay angry with him for the rest of her life to ward off the pain he could cause her? Or would she learn to accept it as part and parcel of loving him?

For her sanity's sake, she knew she would have to go on as before—just simply being herself. She was no actress. She had never known the need to hide her feelings. And why should she? she thought with a spurt of belligerence. She had a right to them.

But one thing was certain. She must hold back the words . . . for now at least.

She was put to the test the moment she entered the apartment. Terry had already left, and Greg was sitting back on the long settee, wincing with the effort of straightening his leg.

'Well, Kate, aren't you going to come and soothe my fevered brow?'

The sardonic inflection in his tone stabbed her to the quick. She straightened her shoulders in an automatic attempt to ward him off.

'You're the one who could do without the wifely gestures. Remember?' she threw over her shoulder as she strode past him. She did not want him to see the gathering tears behind her eyes. But he caught hold of her wrist as she flew past.

'Terry tells me you were upset when the hospital rang.' Kate closed her eyes in despair at his casual statement. Damn Terry! 'I only asked them to contact you to stop you worrying when I was late. Why the tears, Kate?'

'Heaven knows!' she burst out furiously. 'I had this vision of you lying mangled somewhere and for some obscure reason, it happened to upset me!' Her lips clamped shut in an effort to stop them trembling. Greg exerted the little pressure necessary to pull her down beside him.

His long hands framed her face, probing eyes searching her features for the answer to whatever question he was silently asking. Then he lowered his head and brushed his lips tenderly over hers, effortlessly parting them, kissing her so gently in a way that caused her heart to drum a quick tattoo.

'I'm sorry for what I said, Kate,' he said heavily. 'You must know by now I don't possess the best of dispositions.'

'I—it's all right,' she muttered into his throat. The relief of having him here, beside her, well, if not exactly fit, overcame all other emotions for the present.

They lay huddled close for a long time, Greg stroking the nape of her neck through her thick waves and occasionally brushing a fleeting kiss across the top of her head. Kate felt a great sense of contentment steal over her.

This was what had been totally lacking in their marriage, thus far. All physical contact had been as a prelude to lovemaking in the fullest sense—as if he could not be bothered to touch her unless it would culminate in total mutual satisfaction. But it was something Kate knew she craved.

She was a toucher by nature. Spontaneous hugs and kisses to and from her family were commonplace. Not so with Greg.

Their lack of communication on anything but the sexual level was the first hurdle to overcome, she decided. Remembering their honeymoon, she impulsively challenged him to a game of chess. He accepted with barely a hesitation.

The afternoon and evening passed quietly, with no further upsets. Kate felt as if they were both groping their ways to a new relationship. And for the first time, she did not feel shut out when Greg retired to his study to attend to business.

She knocked at the study door at about ten, to tell him she was going to bed.

'Now, that's the best offer I've received all day!'

'Oh—I didn't . . .' Greg watched as if fascinated while a tide of red climbed and spread over Kate's cheeks. Then he dropped his pen as if tired of the game and rubbed at the back of his neck.

'I'm well aware of that, Kate.' He sighed heavily. 'Go on. I'll be with you shortly.'

'I—er—I brought your painkillers.' She put the bottle of tablets on his desk and left the room, thoughtfully pondering that last long glance. Was he trying to tell her something? He seemed so—lonely suddenly.

She felt the bed depress some half an hour later as Greg's weight settled upon it. He clicked off the bedside lamp and lay back, the pain from his knee obviously having eased a little.

'Why are you pretending to be asleep, Kate?' he asked, his casual voice making her jump. 'It's never stopped me before,' he added with a touch of irony, as her nightgown was thrown to the floor. 'I don't know why you bother with those things.'

Kate protested automatically, albeit weakly. She did not know if she could bear the exquisite pleasure of his lovemaking while she was still reeling from her recent discovery. The dangers of giving herself away in the throes of passion were too great to be ignored. And if anything would bring her hopes to a sudden and painful halt, it was a premature declaration of love.

'No, Greg, please . . .' she gasped as his hands found a particularly sensitive spot. 'Your knee—you'll hurt it!' She held her breath as his hands stilled on her body. She could feel his eyes probing her through the darkness.

'Then give to me, Kate,' he muttered finally. 'Just this once. Give!'

She met his kiss half-way with the strangest presentiment that she was undergoing some sort of test. And then there was no place for thoughts . . . only feelings . . .

'Damn!' Greg bit out a muffled oath, slumping against her as the pain in his knee overcame his desire. He lay on his back, sweating profusely, striving to control the pain. Tenderly Kate reached out a hand to wipe his brow, but he brushed it aside impatiently.

'Don't fuss! I'll be all right in a minute!' he snarled, though his statement was negated a moment later as he again attempted to move over her.

'Stop being an idiot, Greg! You can't possibly take your weight on that knee!' she cried, anxious at the pallor of his damp skin.

'You don't for a moment suppose I'm going to be able to sleep like this, do you?'

Kate, accustomed now to the darkness, let her eyes travel the length of his aroused body and, impulsively, she laid a hand on his flat stomach, feeling the muscle clench spasmodically under her massaging fingers.

'For pity's sake, Kate! Don't make it worse!'

In reply, she laid her soft lips against his damp hair-roughened chest, her tongue flicking over the tight male nipples.

'I'm trying to make it better,' she breathed huskily as her

lips journeyed upwards.

A groan issued deep in his throat. 'Kate—Kate, you don't know what you're doing!'

Kate continued on her destructive path, loving the soft tortured moans, the erratic tenor of his breathing.

His whole body went rigid with shock when she finally moved to sit astride him, blindly allowing instinct to guide her down to him. He gave a hoarse moan of pleasure as their bodies merged. She was thankful for the blanket of darkness which shielded her blushing shyness from the man she loved. The man she was being allowed to make love to for the first time.

Not to be outdone, Greg reached out to cup her breasts, drawing her softness down to the hard wall of his chest.

'Kate . . .' Her name was uttered on a tortured breath. She lifted her head from her absorption in the feel of his skin against her lips, the taste of him on her tongue.

'I'm not hurting you, am I?'

He laughed harshly. 'Hurting me? You're torturing me, Kate, I—Oh——' He gripped her hips convulsively, grinding her against him as they found their rhythm. He groaned her name over and over as waves of pleasure overcame them simultaneously.

Slowly, with the greatest reluctance, Kate disentangled herself to lie on her side next to him, but he drew her head down to the comfort of his chest, tenderly caressing her nape. Never had she felt such peace as they lay entwined in the aftermath of their explosion. Thoughts of her own pleasure had not entered her mind. She had given everything she had to offer and in so doing had discovered her new-found love had added a further dimension to lovemaking she had already thought perfect. But now she knew Greg's pleasure was her own.

'Why did you do that, Kate?' he whispered, a note of awe still present in his voice.

'Didn't you like it?' she teased, not wanting to spoil this magic moment with a post-mortem. He took his cue from her, pressing her shoulder lightly.

'So much, my love. So much!' The softly spoken

endearment reverberated through her mind. Greg did not use such words lightly, as would Terry or her family. Kate was a little reserved herself in her use of them. But she could not recall Greg doing it before even in the heat of passion. But if those two little words gave her cause for hope, his next statement warmed her even further.

'Caroline never stayed here, you know.'

Her breath stilled, then left her in a rush. 'Thank you,' was all she could say. She felt well rewarded for her gift of herself. He had known all along what had prompted her to redecorate their room so completely—and he did not mind! 'Can you sleep now?'

He expelled his breath on a long, long sigh. 'Yes, Kate, I shall sleep now.'

But it was a long time before sleep claimed Kate. She lay for hours staring at Greg's features, so relaxed and vulnerable in repose. The lines on his forehead were smoothed out and his preposterously long eyelashes fanned over his high cheekbones. Even his mouth, so hard and cynical in his waking moments, looked softer as he slept. The low, steady rhythm of his breathing was a pleasure in itself to Kate, since it was she who had enabled him to rest.

Her fingers itched to run through the dark hair so close to hers, but she restrained the urge. Just as she had resisted the temptation to tell him of her love. Now was not the time. A man like Greg would need proof, and it was up to her to supply all the evidence he would need.

She knew she would never again resist his lovemaking—but would give herself to him with all the warmth and passion inherent in her nature—as, she now admitted, she had longed to do from the second day of their marriage.

'I'll prove to you that love exists, my darling,' she promised his sleeping form. 'If it takes all the days of the rest of our lives, I'll prove it.'

During the next few weeks, Kate sometimes had to stifle the growing hope that Greg did, indeed, care more for her than he was willing to admit. Since that never-to-be-forgotten night when she had finally given herself to him, their relationship

had undergone a subtle but definite change. The evening
conferences which had so consumed her time before she married
Greg were a thing of the past. She did not question the extra
hours she had with her husband, just quietly revelled in the
pleasure of his company.

And it was a pleasure. The quiet, undemanding, comfortable
pleasure she had always believed to be at the very foundation of
a successful marriage.

Neither of them were social creatures. They exchanged small
dinner parties with Sam and Marie fairly frequently, there were
occasional cinema or theatre visits or quiet meals out, but mostly
their evenings were spent at the apartment, feeling their way to a
new, closer relationship.

Their lovemaking took on a tenderness and spontaneity totally
lacking before, and despite all Kate's efforts to douse it, a small
flame of hope began burning brighter by the day.

She had decided, after some thought, that any overt moves to
cement their new closeness should be made by Greg. That was
part shrewdness and part cowardice, but Kate was anxious not
to ruin everything by precipitate action. What they had now was
so much more than she had expected in the dark days after Greg
had made his intentions clear. So she played the cards as they
were dealt her, taking each day as it came.

Until the day matters were taken firmly out of her control by
an event Kate—or, for that matter, Greg—should have foreseen.

One morning, about six weeks after Greg's accident, he
returned unexpectedly, having left his car keys behind. He had
left Kate snoozing in bed, that being one of her days at home.
He found her slumped lethargically on the bathroom floor,
overcome with nausea.

'Kate—darling!' His voice was anguished, but Kate was too
miserable to notice. Weakly she laid her head against his chest as
he scooped her into his arms, the quickened thud of his
heartbeats sounding reassuringly in her ear. He laid her on the
bed and tenderly wiped a faint film of perspiration from her
brow.

'Don't move, love. I'm going to call the doctor.'
Darling—love. Two endearments in as many seconds. Words
which at any other time would have filled her heart with joy.

But now . . .? Kate held on to him as he would have turned to the phone, terrified that the news she had no choice but to impart would turn him back into the cold, hard man she had married. Nerving herself for the confrontation, she pulled out of his embrace.

She had berated herself over and over for her foolhardy lack of foresight. To overlook something as basic as birth control was almost criminal in this day and age. Children were a subject they had never touched upon. She had no idea how Greg would feel about such an upheaval in both their lives. In fact she had no idea if he had intended their marriage to be a permanent arrangement. But even as she steeled herself to break the news, she could not be sorry. Already she loved the tiny flicker of life inside her—no matter how sick it made her feel. She kept her eyes fixed firmly on his tie as she whispered shakily, 'There's no point in calling a doctor, Greg.'

'Don't be silly, Kate,' he teased her, the light in his eyes warming her—for the moment. 'It's obvious something is wrong.'

'No.' Her voice was still cracked. She blinked hard and moistened her dry lips with the tip of her tongue. 'That is—there's nothing wrong exactly.' She looked up in time to catch his dawning comprehension and nodded wearily. 'It's too early to confirm.' She shrugged her shoulders helplessly and averted her eyes, unwilling to see the condemnation she knew he must be feeling as she tonelessly recited her symptoms. 'I'm a couple of weeks overdue, and I've been sick the last three mornings.' Still he said nothing. Stealing a glance from beneath her lashes, she surprised a strange expression flitting across his face, one she had seen before when she was awaiting his judgement on the newly decorated bedroom. Acting on impulse, as she had done so often these past weeks, she scrambled on her knees to the edge of the bed so she could lay her hands on his shoulders and force him to meet the sincerity in her eyes.

'I didn't do it deliberately, Greg. You must believe that. I just didn't think . . .' Her voice broke off, shoulders slumping in defeat at his continued silence. Then, incredibly, he spoke.

'I believe you, Kate.' She looked up, hope rising within her, to see his eyes crinkle in wry amusement, as if he were laughing at a joke against himself. 'Amazingly enough, I never gave it a thought either. And, of the two of us, I'm the most experienced.' And then she didn't hear another word, for she flung herself into his arms, at last being able to give way to the joy of having created a new life, laughter and tears making her incoherent, until he gently put her from him and mopped up the worst of the waterfall.

'Don't worry, Kate. Things will work out. I'll make an appointment with the doctor when I get to the office. You feeling all right now?' She smiled tremulously, reassuring him, and he bestowed a gentle kiss on her parted lips, then turned abruptly, as he always did after a show of what she imagined he called weakness. 'By the way,' he threw over his shoulder as he reached the door, 'you'd better start looking for a house. It seems we're going to need a garden.'

Her breath was suspended, leaving her gaping open-mouthed until the click of the outer door signalled Greg's departure. Then she literally clapped her hands in sheer happiness and jumped off the bed to dance an impulsive pirouette—regretting it instantly as she was forced to dash to the bathroom again.

The two dozen red roses which arrived three hours later restored her to full and vibrant life.

The following days were filled with such happiness that Kate forgot to be on her guard. Her parents, Sam and Marie, Terry and his latest centrefold were invited to a special celebration, and every time Kate met Greg's watchful eyes her heart would nearly burst with the simple delight she found in his presence. He must know I love him, she thought dazedly sometimes. I can feel it written all over me, so surely he can see it. But it did not matter. She no longer feared his derision, for day by day her suspicion that he loved her grew into certainty.

His remoteness had almost faded completely; it was surely only a matter of time before he openly declared himself—and if he didn't, well, Kate had begun work on a project guaranteed to force him out into the open. Soon she knew she would be handed the icing on an already delicious cake!

Precisely three weeks later, she found the house of her dreams. The house she knew she could turn into a home where she could happily spend the rest of her life. With Greg.

Mr Brownlea, the estate agent recommended to her, had been nearing despair. He was a very dignified man with unlimited patience, but Kate sadly upset all his preconceived ideas of how the young wife of a rich executive should conduct herself. Worse still, she had absolutely no compunction about stating exactly what she thought of the most exclusive properties on his books. Not one of them had received more than a cursory glance before being dismissed out of hand as too new, too old, too flamboyant, too trendy, too twee, too ugly or too pretty.

He did, however, admire her boundless energy and her determination to find the perfect home. Though his suspicion that she was—to put it kindly—a trifle eccentric was proved beyond a shadow of a doubt when her choice was made.

It was after three weeks of fruitlessly searching the Midlands, and with the horrifying sensation of a large chunk of commission slipping through his fingers, that he came up with what he hoped might be an acceptable solution.

With the tact and diplomacy peculiar only to estate agents, he suggested the possibility of building a house to her own design.

'I have the perfect plot of land on my books at the moment. A most delightful setting—Inkberrow, Worcestershire. We did pass through it the other day, if you recall.'

Kate recalled only too well. Unfortunately she also recalled the unbelievably ugly monstrosity he had intended her to view. Her polite listening face began to crumble with a recurring vision of her presiding over the local WI—but the expression of gloom settling on Mr Brownlea's already lugubrious features made her think again.

He really was rather a dear, and Kate knew she had been a sore trial to **him**. It surely wouldn't hurt to just look, would it?

'The dwelling currently situated on the site would naturally have to be demolished. It would cost far more to restore than to build new. Besides,' a decided twinkle made an appearance in a still serious face, 'it's rather a white elephant of a place. Though I'd be grateful if you didn't repeat that,' he added hastily as Kate laughed, delighted to find the man possessed a sense of humour after all—a trait put severely to the test when she fell in love with that very same white elephant the instant she set eyes on it!

* * *

Unable to contain her excitement, Kate pounced on Greg the second he entered the apartment that evening. Sheets of paper flew every which way to join the huge floor plans set out on the carpet. Poor Mr Brownlea, still not certain whether or not she was serious, had been handed a tape measure and together they had taken measurements throughout the ramshackle house—despite the misgivings the estate agent had about the safety of the floorboards. Kate had no such worries. The house was solid—she just knew it.

'Oh, darling!' She flung her arms about Greg's neck, completely missing his astonished reaction to such a fervent greeting. 'I've found it—the perfect house! And what do you think? That pompous little twit from the estate agents said it would have to be demolished!' Her breasts heaved with indignation at the thought of such sacrilege. Then she giggled as she remembered the dazed look on Mr Brownlea's face when he had finally managed to drag her away from the house. 'I do believe the poor man thinks I'm quite mad!'

'And why's that?' Greg shrugged off his jacket and loosened his tie.

'Well, it does need a little restoration work . . .' Honesty won out. She took a deep breath and plunged in. 'Make that rather a lot of restoration work.'

'Such as?' he cut in indulgently as soon as he could interrupt the flow. Kate looked at him lovingly. Such warm grey eyes——How could she ever have thought them cold? 'Kate . . .?' he prompted gently, putting an arm across her shoulders to propel her into the lounge.

'It needs rewiring.'

'No problem. And . . .?'

'Replastering and redecorating throughout.'

'No problem. And . . .?'

Her lips twitched. 'A new roof.'

He sighed. 'And . . .?'

'And a few walls knocked down here and there.'

Greg's eyelids hooded his expression, but Kate took heart from the small smile playing around his mouth—and those brows were aimed upwards!

'I think I need a drink,' he murmured drily.

'Oh, I'll get it!' She jumped up quickly—too quickly. Her head swam and she would have fallen had Greg not reached her in time.

'Dammit, Kate, I warned you about doing too much! Sit down—I'll see to the drinks!'

'I think I'd better stick to fruit juice.' She essayed a reassuring smile, but Greg's expression remained grim. 'I haven't been doing too much, Greg, honestly. I——' she bit her lip nervously, praying that his good mood would return. He was going to need it! 'I just got up too quickly, that's all.' He handed her a pineapple juice which she sipped gratefully.

'I don't think this house is a good idea, Kate. Hell, don't look at me like that!' He raked his fingers through his hair, his agitation plain. 'I don't mean forget finding a house altogether. Just this one . . .'

'But this is *the* one, Greg. Just come and see it. Please!'

He stared for long agonising seconds into her glowingly imploring green eyes before succumbing to their appeal.

'All right,' he conceded grudgingly, though he grinned at her relieved sigh. 'But I have to tell you, I had hoped to move into a house, not a building site!'

An hour later Kate was wishing she had prepared the groundwork a little better. She had been so filled with plans of how the house would look, she had forgotten just how broken-down it looked at first sight. She knew she was being a little fanciful, but she had felt a sense of welcome from the very beginning. In spite—or even perhaps because—of its sad state of neglect, the house exuded a homely dignity, one Kate had already transformed in her mind's eye.

As Mr Brownlea had promised, the setting was delightful, if a little overgrown. The orchard attached to the land had become a veritable jungle.

And the house——The original colour was hard to distinguish and most of the—possibly—red tiles from the roof were dotted haphazardly around the grounds. There was not a window left intact—obviously the local children had had a field day throwing stones. It was also impossible to describe the house as regards its shape. It was very irregular, portions having been added here and there with little regard for aesthetics. Kate thought it charming.

The interior was, if anything, worse. Greg said not one word as she showed him around, save one unsuitable for repetition when he caught sight of the magnificent clawed feet of the rusty bath. Kate dawdled miserably behind him as he stood scanning the overgrown landscape. She could sense the anger in him, and quite honestly could not blame him for it.

'You can't possibly be serious, Kate! No one in their right mind would actually want to live in this dump!' He gestured forcibly. 'It's falling down!'

'Greg . . .'

'It's impossible!' Kate flinched at the curt tone. It had been so long since she had heard it, she had forgotten the power it had to hurt her. Greg sighed wearily, passing a hand over his taut face. 'Why do you always make me feel a heel when I have to say no?'

'Let me show you something, Greg.' She had to try one more time. The idea of building them a home had assumed too much importance for her to dismiss it without a fight. 'Please let me show you what I have in mind?' She held her breath until his curt nod gave her permission to run to the car to retrieve her sketchbook.

They found a couple of crates in the garden and perched precariously while she made lightning sketches of how she envisaged all the rooms.

'Now, we have three storeys here——' She chewed thoughtfully on her pencil, lost in the transformation her sketches had brought to life. 'The top floor, I thought we could use for the nursery suite—there's a couple of good-sized bedrooms, a bath could be installed there——' she pointed towards an archway between rooms. 'And in the middle here, we could have a giant playroom. There's plenty of space for some sort of games room later on—snooker, table tennis, whatever. The master bedroom suite would be directly underneath. The rooms are massive there, so there won't be any need to knock any walls through. As a matter of fact, we may have to build some sort of divider.' Greg muttered something under his breath, but Kate, well into her stride, continued regardless. 'We can make two guest bedrooms there—with a bathroom between them, perhaps. That room there could be used as a dressing-room—or another bathroom, if you like. It would lead straight into the master bedroom. There's a great gallery landing—once that window is enlarged, the light will be fantastic. Likewise, the stairs will have to be opened up. 'And the ground floor . . .'

'Stop a minute!' Greg laid a hand over hers, staring down at the sketches. Kate remained motionless, not even looking at him for fear he would refuse her. She could sense a inner battle raging within him, he was so tense. After what seemed hours, but was in reality less than a minute, she heard him expel a breath on a long sigh.

'Two conditions . . .' She looked up sharply. His face gave nothing away, though he continued to stare at the sketches as if mesmerised. 'If you're going to involve yourself in this, then Susan will take over your job full-time.'

'I . . .' Kate started to object, more out of habit than anything. Was her job so important? Important enough to lose this home? She would be forced to leave in another few months in any case, to care for the baby. She had never been so career-orientated that she would insist on working no matter what. It wasn't as if they needed the money . . . Cautiously, she nodded agreement.

'Very well. There are still a few things to be tied up and . . .' the desire not to capitulate totally made her rebel—just a little, 'I can still help you in the evenings, can't I?'

'Depending on how you feel,' he compromised.

'OK. And the other thing?'

'The surveyor's report. If he says no, I don't want to hear another word.'

How Kate stopped herself blurting out the words of love which sprang to her lips she would never know. The house was as good as theirs. If she could convince Greg, that most practical of men, then what had she to fear from a surveyor?

Within a week they had the report. And it was all systems go! Kate dragged Greg to the estate agents at the first opportunity, eager to begin work on their new home. The only drawback was that they would have to continue living in the apartment until at least after the baby's birth, which was a pity, but could not be helped. Kate intended to ensure that the wait would be worth while. Besides, the apartment didn't seem so bad now. Though she still did not feel truly at home there.

She had once had the fanciful notion that Greg's nature was influenced by his surroundings. If so, then their future together would lack for nothing, because she intended their home to be the very antithesis of the apartment. Warmth and comfort would be the overriding factor all through the house.

Even Mr Brownlea could not dampen her enthusiasm today. Kate derived a great deal of amusement from the man's obvious relief at having so level-headed a man as Greg to deal with, her smile broadening when Greg winked at her in recognition of the detailed caricature she had provided.

'Now, sir—madam,' the professional smile faltered as it encountered Kate's bland stare, as if not sure what the madwoman would come up with next. It was very clear where his sympathies lay—especially after Greg had proved himself eminently practical regarding mortgage arrangements. He cleared his throat. 'If I may recommend a few firms to carry out the renovations?' At their smiles of agreement, he continued, 'Let me see—you'll need landscapers, builders, plumbers, electricians, carpenters, interior designers . . .'

Kate interrupted sharply.

'No interior designers.' She intercepted a sardonic look from Greg, knowing too well he was thinking of Caroline Sterling. But her decision had nothing to do with his old girlfriend. Kate merely felt strongly enough about the house to need to be involved with the whole project rather than just handing it all over to a professional body. 'I'll be responsible for that.'

'Well, the work will be rather extensive, Mrs Courtney. And if I might suggest, a little too much, considering your—ahem—condition.'

Kate glared at the estate agent. 'I think that's for me to decide, Mr Brownlea.'

'Nevertheless, Mr Brownlea does have a point, Kate,' Greg stated with a frown. 'I didn't realise you meant to oversee the whole operation.'

'Not merely oversee, Greg.' Green eyes flashed with a spark of defiance reserved for subjects dear to her heart. 'There's no reason why I shouldn't do some of the decorating myself. I know Mom . . .'

'Like hell you will!' Greg exploded so suddenly that Mr Brownlea actually jumped. Regardless of the older man's horrified expression, he rose to tower over Kate, his eyes as hard as agate. 'If you think I'll allow my wife . . . my pregnant wife . . .'

They both turned at the sound of a discreet cough, Mr Brownlea's anxious expression giving them both pause. Greg breathed deeply. 'Do forgive us, Mr Brownlea. My wife tends to take me by surprise on occasion.'

The men's shared grimace of masculine commiseration did nothing to soothe Kate's ruffled feathers, but she wisely bit back the hasty words she suddenly longed to throw at them. There was too much at stake to lose her temper when a little sweet reason should work in her favour.

'Perhaps you could get in touch with me later on. There's plenty of time, after all.'

'Good idea, Mr Brownlea. Thank you for your assistance. Good morning.'

Greg had her out of the office and strapped into the Mercedes before she had time to draw breath.

'What the hell do you mean, you'll be doing the decorating yourself?' he demanded angrily as he drew into the line of traffic.

'There's nothing to get worked up about, Greg. I can plan the colour schemes without having to leave the apartment. Shops will send samples of curtain and carpet materials. As for the actual decorating . . .' she swallowed a nervous lump in her throat, 'I was planning to ask Mom and perhaps Terry to help. We did a good job on the bedroom, didn't we?'

'That's not the point. You weren't pregnant then.'

Kate stole a look at his profile, then wished she hadn't. There was a set, determined look on his face which boded ill for anyone crossing him. But she had to at least try.

'It's mainly the nursery suite I wanted to do myself . . .'

'Let's get one thing clear right now, Kate.' Greg, stopping at a red light, was able to turn and face her. 'There is no way I will permit you to climb ladders in your condition. In case you've forgotten, I do have a half-share in this baby.'

'But, Greg . . .'

'No, Kate.'

She turned to stare out of the side window, reluctance to argue warring with resentment at his high-handedness.

'There's nothing to stop you doing the high bits . . .' she muttered in a mutinous tone. The tense silence caused her to turn and surprise a harsh glint in his eyes as he stared at her incredulously.

'Are you trying to domesticate me, Kate?' he rasped, a grimly suspicious set to his jawline.

Her eyes opened wide in hurt confusion. What had she done? Surely it was not so inconceivable that he should wield a paintbrush? She knew her family would be happy enough to help out. And Terry. Why not Greg? They could have such fun renovating the house.

'No, Greg, I wouldn't dream of it.' Her voice wobbled slightly, tears not far away. 'I'm just trying to make us a home. I'm sorry you find the idea so objectionable.'

His only reply was a disbelieving grunt. The drive home was completed in silence.

And Kate was made to realise their relationship was more fragile than she had thought.

She turned hesitantly towards him as he pulled up outside their apartment block to drop her off before making his way to work.

'I—er—will you be home at the usual time?'

'Why?' He glared the question at her. She swallowed the ball of disillusionment threatening to choke her, her lower lip betraying how near tears were to falling. Her pregnancy had appeared to heighten any emotional state somewhat, so the depression falling upon her now was in direct proportion to the happiness she had become accustomed to over the past few weeks.

'I've invited Sam and Marie for dinner,' she told him.

Greg's impatient oath was the last straw. She thrust open the car door and scrambled out, stopping only to throw at him, 'I only asked them because it's your damned birthday tomorrow. Normal people like their friends' company at such a time!'

She slammed the car door shut with scant regard for the paintwork and stormed up the three flights of stairs, disdaining use of the lift.

She would have walked straight past Terry, who was squatting outside the apartment, had he not spoken.

'Hey, love, what's up?' He looked alarmed at Kate's stormy features as she strove to regain her breath enough to greet him. 'You look as if you've a pack of hounds at your heels!'

'I probably have.' She pulled a face as she searched her handbag for a doorkey, cursing the amount of rubbish she had to plough through before finding it. 'Come on in. I think we've still got some beer left—I might even join you!'

'No time, love, I'm sorry. But I'm on my way to Inverness.' He checked his watch. 'Matter of fact, I should have been on my way an hour ago. But I thought I'd better give you this.' He handed her a package. 'I'm not sure what time I'll be back tomorrow, so . . .'

Kate looked despondently at the package. She knew exactly what it contained—her birthday gift for Greg. The final proof of her love for him. She had pinned such hopes on it, ninety-nine per cent certain her gift would be welcomed. But now . . .?

'Don't tell me you've changed your mind?' Terry burst out in exasperation as she took the package with miserable reluctance. Her expression spoke volumes. 'Hell, princess! You've been dithering about this for weeks. You have to tell him—you know that. And if you don't, then I will!'

'No!' Kate paled at the thought. 'Please, Terry! Promise me you won't?'

Ever since she had confided in him on the day of Greg's accident, Terry had been urging her to tell Greg how she felt. Terry was so straightforward, so uncomplicated, Kate had not been able to make him fully understand the complexities of the situation.

'I have to pick the right moment, Terry.'

'All right!' The promise was dragged from him. 'But for heaven's sake get this damn thing settled once and for all, will you?' His voice softened then, Kate's tearful face causing him to gather her close for a bearlike hug. 'I love you, princess. I want you to be happy. And you won't be, either of you, until you face up to the truth.' He bent and kissed her forehead gently.

CHAPTER TEN

TERRY'S cheery certainty failed to have its normal bolstering effect on her flagging spirits as Kate let herself into the empty apartment. He had helped her a few times whenever the immensity of the gamble she was taking proved a little too nerve-racking. Until this morning, she would have said that the odds were overwhelmingly in her favour. Now she was back to thinking of it as an outside chance at best.

What had gone wrong? Everything had appeared to be exactly on schedule for the culmination of all her cherished hopes and dreams tonight . . .

The thawing of Greg's attitude towards her, begun so dramatically the night of his accident, had continued unabated, so much so that Kate had dropped her guard completely. And though she had never said the words to Greg, neither had she troubled to hide how she felt. If she only had a reason—something to work on . . .

Catching sight of herself in the long hall mirror gave her pause. It surely wasn't possible he was upset about the baby?

Looking at herself critically made her think twice. Although she was just less than four months into her pregnancy, the bulge of her stomach had already forced her into maternity clothes. She clearly remembered her mother laughing about how big she had become with all of her pregnancies, and it would appear Kate was to follow in her footsteps. Was that what was upsetting Greg? That she was undesirable now that her body was becoming misshapen?

No—Kate laid protective hands on her stomach. No—last night had surely proved he still desired her? No man could fake such unabated passion. Besides, it had been their baby which had brought about the greatest change in him.

He had actually begun to treat her as a rare and precious gift since she had broken the news of her pregnancy. Mistily she recalled all those mornings he had brought her tea and arrowroot biscuits to allay the morning sickness—and now that had abated, he still constantly reminded her not to tire herself. She had never felt so—cherished, not even by her mother.

And anyway, though modesty forbade her admitting it out loud, she thought she had never looked better. Her skin had taken on a special bloom, her eyes glowed bright. Even her hair had started behaving itself! And certainly she had never felt better—until now.

The only other thing Kate could think had upset Greg was the house. And that did bring a small twinge of apprehension as she recalled how immersed she had become in drawing up plans over the last week.

And there had been all that hassle of making Greg see what could be done to the house to transform it into a home—a real home, as far removed from this empty shell of an apartment as could be.

In fact—Kate went to search out her growing portfolio of sketches, recalling the evening they had returned home after first viewing the house. Greg had been in an odd mood then, she remembered, and, thinking he was brooding on the wisdom of his decision to let her go ahead, she had drawn a large sketch of the house—transformed according to her dreams.

Ah yes, there it was. She drew it out of the portfolio and forced herself to study it objectively, and was alarmed to see how she had romanticised it. She had even drawn a sunset in the background, for heaven's sake! But even so, she could not believe it a valid reason for his attempt to distance himself now. If he had objections, he would have voiced them at the time. Unless . . .

Kate chewed absently at her lower lip. Unless he was feeling neglected? She had spent a long time on the portfolio. And come to think of it, they had barely touched on any other subject all week.

Even when they had visited Sam and Marie four days previously, Kate had enthusiastically regaled Marie with every last detail, Marie's interest fuelling her own.

'Nest building,' Marie had called it when Kate shyly

described the feeling of welcome she had experienced at first sight of the house, as if the bricks and mortar had been impatiently awaiting her arrival. She had been so immersed in her theme she had not sought Greg's reaction. Had her thoughts become so focused on the house that she had failed Greg in some way? It was all too possible.

With an impulsive resolution, she grabbed her purse and shopping bag, mentally altering the menu she had planned for that evening. Tonight she would put a favourite maxim of her mother's to the test! 'The way to a man's heart is through his stomach'. Just let him try and feel neglected after she had finished with him! Kate thought, with the inevitable blush, or rather a novel idea for dessert! Of course, she would have to think of something else to serve to Sam and Marie!

The phone was ringing when she re-entered the apartment several pounds poorer, and she hurried over to answer it thinking—hoping, that it was Greg.

She was mistaken.

Just how mistaken, about everything, was still tormenting her half an hour later when she called Marie to cancel their dinner arrangements.

It was a difficult conversation. It had been the great sadness of the Goodises' lives that they had been unable to have children of their own. Greg had filled that gap to some extent and Kate, especially now that she was pregnant, had been taken firmly under their joint protective wing. But Marie finally accepted Kate's excuse of tiredness without imagining anything too catastrophic.

For how could she tell Marie the real truth? With the bitter gall of failure rising to her throat, Kate could imagine the conversation as it would have been:

'Sorry, Marie, I can't have you to dinner . . . You see, I've just discovered Greg has hired his ex-mistress to design the interior of our new house—of what was to have been our home—knowing, of course, how I feel about it, and her—and her damned cold designs. Knowing it could—would destroy everything good between us. And I won't be able to pretend that everything is wonderful, not even for you, because my heart's never been broken before, and I don't know how to cope with it . . .'

Much later, like an old woman crippled by pain, Kate slowly made her way to the bedroom, the only room in the apartment bearing her own personality. On the lounge floor she left the litter of her dreams—all her plans, her designs for the home she would never see outside her imagination. A sudden attack of nausea forced her into the bathroom.

The retching left her weak and giddy. She slumped to the floor and rested her hot forehead against the cool wall tiles, feeling too wretched to move—even when she heard the sound of the outer door opening.

She came slowly back to full consciousness when a damp flannel was passed over her forehead and she raised listless eyes to Greg's impassive features. Her lover of the last few weeks was nowhere in sight, only the cold-eyed, enigmatically sardonic stranger she had married.

If she had harboured the tiniest of hopes that Caroline Sterling had lied to her on the phone, they were dashed in that instant. But still her skin burnt where he touched her and she roused herself enough to push him violently away.

'Don't you touch me!'

Her eyes, the only trace of colour in her ashen face, blazed green fire at him, but there was no visible reaction to her blatant misery. Tight-lipped, Greg turned on his heel and marched from the bathroom.

Grimly Kate strove to embrace the hazy numbness beginning to anaesthetise her mind, and forced her trembling limbs to carry her back into the bedroom.

'Do you need a doctor?' Greg asked with icy impersonal concern the moment she made an entrance. 'Marie was concerned about you,' he added when she did not answer.

'No, I do not need a doctor.' Her voice was as pale as her face.

'You were sick . . .'

'Your girlfriend tends to have that effect on people,' she returned calmly—too calmly.

His brows lowered to an ominous level. Kate couldn't have given a damn. 'She was rather upset at the way you spoke to her.'

'I can't remember saying above two words.'

'From what Caroline tells me, they were more than enough.'

'Well, I'm sure you consoled her. I take it there's no point in trying to persuade you to change your mind?'

Even as his expression answered her question, Kate realised it would be a waste of time. Her objections would be the last thing to be taken into consideration. After all, it was only her life being torn apart.

'It's only a house, Kate,' Greg stated quietly, shrugging off her misery as of no account. 'Why all the fuss?'

'And why, from the scores of firms you could have chosen if you were so intent on bringing in professional help, did you settle on the one most likely to hurt me?'

One brow rose, deriding her conclusion.

'Rather melodramatic, don't you think?' He shrugged again, his eyes glittering over her pale sad face. 'I simply prefer her designs to yours. Nothing personal, you understand?'

A swift sharp stab of pain hurtled through the numbness and held her motionless. His cold scrutiny brought a terrible bleak emptiness to her face.

He was lying—she knew that. But the knowledge did not help her one iota. His mind was made up. And Kate knew she could never reconcile herself to living again in the cold emptiness of a marriage as devoid of warmth as a house designed by Caroline Sterling would be.

Not now—now that she knew how it could be . . .

Her neck ached with the effort of holding her head high, but she bravely fought her way through the new access of misery lying in wait for her.

'Fine,' she bit out tightly. 'You have Caroline build you another igloo—you can chill each other to death over the chrome accessories. But count me out, Greg. I need warmth in my home—something to thaw me out after any encounter with you. She'll suit you much better.'

Moving like an automaton, she pulled open the doors of the large walk-in closet built into the wall and dragged out a large suitcase.

'What the hell do you think you're doing?' Greg tore the

case out of her nerveless hand and flung it across the room. 'We made a bargain, Kate.'

Wearily, she turned and drew out another case which went the same way as the first.

'No, Greg. You made the bargain. I was just dragged along for the ride.'

'If you think for a moment that I'll allow you to go from me to Terry, you're making a very grave——'

'What did you say?' Incredulous, Kate began to back away from him, recoiling in horror from the raw anger devouring him.

'Oh, so innocent!' he rasped harshly, his lips twisting in vicious contempt. 'So sweet, so caring, so bloody loving! And it was all a sham, wasn't it?' The words were ground out through tightly clenched teeth, his hands jammed tight into his trouser pockets as if he were afraid to let them loose.

The emotionless mask had finally cracked with a vengeance. And it was too late . . .

As bitterly unhappy as she had been before, Kate had not felt anger. But now it took flight. How dared he? Terry had told her Greg was jealous of him, but she had never believed it. She did not believe it now. It was all an excuse—an excuse to push her away. An excuse for his own inability to give her anything he could not buy.

And still his foul accusations rent the air between them.

'Don't bother to deny it, Kate. I heard him—this morning, remember? I actually had the crazy idea I'd upset you, so I came chasing after you to find you in his arms. "I love you, princess"!' His voice was a savage mimicry of Terry's. '"I want you to be happy". And you, Kate? How do you feel? Are his feelings reciprocated? Tell me, dammit!'

The open-handed slap she delivered caught them both by surprise. Throwing any remnants of caution to the wind, she flung back her head, meeting his murderous glare head-on.

'You miserable bastard! What the hell has it ever mattered to you how I feel? But just for the record—yes, Terry loves me. Just as I love him. He gives me something you're incapable of even feeling! Friendship, Greg—ever heard of it? Ever experienced it? No—you can't, can you?' she sneered as icily as with any callous remark he had casually thrown her way during their brief marriage. 'Can't have the great self-sufficient Gregory Courtney actually needing someone, can we? To need to confide in someone? To share, to laugh—to even, heaven forbid! asking a favour of someone? No, that would mean having to give part of yourself in return, wouldn't it?' This time it was Greg who backed away from stark fury. 'Have you ever given anything of yourself, Greg? Even to Sam and Marie? Yes, I know you rewarded them financially—you can't bear to be beholden——' She passed a hand over her face. 'I doubt if you even know the difference.'

She exhaled slowly, the anger draining away with the breath, to be replaced by a misery so acute she could feel it begin to claw at her. She was so tired.

'I'm the daughter of Terry's best friend, Greg. He's loved me since I was nine years old. Just as I've loved him. Just as Sam and Marie have loved you. Nothing more, nothing less. Oh lord!' Wearily she sank on to the bed, burying her face in her hands. 'I don't know why I'm bothering to explain. This has nothing to do with any imaginary infidelity.' She kept her face averted. 'You've been looking for an excuse ever since we found the house, haven't you? Why, Greg? Why does the concept of a real home frighten you?'

'I don't know what you're talking about.' The lowering brows were an automatic reflex.

'No, I don't suppose you do,' she whispered sadly, a wistful curve to her pale lips. 'You really should have married Caroline, Greg. It would have saved you all the trouble of turning me into a duplicate of her. That's what you wanted, wasn't it? Someone you could keep at a distance? Someone who would be content with the things you could give her without asking for feelings too? I won't let you do that to me.'

'Just what am I supposed to think when I see you and Terry embracing in the hallway? When I see him hand you gifts?' Greg went straight for the jugular, disregarding her explanation. But Kate had already gone through the pain barrier. Nothing he said now could hurt her any more.

'You're supposed to remember who I am, what I am. You're supposed to remember how we made love last night. You're supposed to know how impossible it would be for me to give myself to you if I were betraying you. That's what I had to do when Caroline rang me. Don't you think I had good reason to believe you intended taking up with her again? But I know, because of who you are and the promise you made me, that you wouldn't be physically unfaithful to me.' There was no emotion left in her voice, just a sad reflection of what might have been. Even so, she was wasting her time.

Greg wasn't listening to her. He was watching as she automatically folded a few things into her suitcase, her precise actions pouring fuel on the flames of his anger.

'Damn you, Kate!' He jerked her around as she opened another drawer. 'You're going nowhere!'

'I have to go! I can't stay here any longer.' She looked around her, the pleasure she had once found in this one room of the apartment dissipating to leave it as cold as the rest. Her head was lifted until her mouth was a whisper away from his, his compelling sexuality drawing her into him despite her despair.

'I could force you to stay here, Kate. We both know that.' Her eyelids fluttered down to protect her from the metallic glitter demanding her surrender.

'I've never denied it, Greg. But if you still feel any of that liking or respect you once said you had for me then you'll let me go, because I can't bear this half-marriage any longer.'

The stark honesty of her weary reply stunned him. For once in his life he was at a complete and utter loss. Despite the speed with which his mind worked he could think of nothing to stop her—save one. One far too dangerous to even contemplate.

'Very well, Kate. I—I apologise if I've over-reacted . . . But you have to admit that takes some explaining.' He gestured towards the package Terry had delivered. It was lying in open view in the drawer she had just started to empty. 'And when do I get to hear that secret you're waiting for the right time to divulge?'

The breath caught painfully in her throat. Had she possessed the energy then hysterics beckoned enticingly. Oh yes, she had been waiting, planning, yearning for the right time. Somehow, this little scene was not at all what she had had in mind.

But the luxury of hysterics would have to be denied. She needed all the energy she could conserve. Her baby would need it. She would need it—when she left.

There was no other way but to leave. All that had sustained her throughout the months of her marriage had been the hope and then the certainty that Greg loved her. She had now been stripped of both. If she were to retain any sense of self-worth to pass on to her child, then it was imperative she remove herself from the temptation of Greg's presence. And, with the clarity of vision visited upon people at such a time of extreme distress, she knew there was only one way to escape him. One reason he would let her go before he destroyed more than her dreams.

She retrieved the lovingly wrapped package and handed it to him.

'This—this is what I was waiting to tell you. Open it, Greg.'

His head jerked up, eyes questioning her.

'My birthday present? I don't understand . . .'

'You will when you open it.'

She sat beside him on the bed as, in slow motion, as if reluctant to reveal the secret, he carefully unwrapped the gift, drawing in a sharp painful breath at the sight of his own image staring back at him.

It was clear from the shocked revelation written on his white face that he was recalling what she had once said to him—that she could only sketch portraits of people she loved.

'I knew you would need proof, you see. You wouldn't have believed the words . . . Terry got it framed for me. I . . .' She could not go on. His silence was eloquently informing her that she had been mistaken all along. He might care for her in his own fashion. But he did not love her—not as Kate understood the word.

And all the time he simply sat there, staring at his own face. It really was an incredibly good sketch—better even than those of her family. The eyes, alive with that faintly quizzical air, as if he were questioning himself along with everyone around him. One well-defined brow was raised, and there was a cynical smile playing around his lips. She had seen that expression so often lately, and had misinterpreted it completely. She had put too much warmth in the eyes, she could see that now. Funny how it had come so naturally at the time . . .

She swallowed once—twice, then tried to speak. Nothing more than a husky whisper could force itself past the tight constriction in her throat.

'So you see . . . you see, I have to leave, Greg. You—this marriage—it's destroying me. I can't . . .' She breathed deeply, not even sure he was listening to her. He was so very still, his fingers wrapped tautly around the gilt frame of the portrait. 'I have to leave before I give in to the temptation to become the sort of person you want me to be. I—you want me to give up the part of myself which makes me who I am.'

'Yes, I know. I can see . . .' He cleared his throat, though he still spoke as if to himself. 'All this time I thought I was protecting you . . . I'm sorry, Kate, more sorry than I can say.' He looked at her and flinched at her broken expression. The skin was stretched tightly over his well-sculpted cheekbones—a path she had traced so very many times. 'You're absolutely correct, of course. I can't go on hurting you in this way.'

And Kate's last, lingering hope died a swift and excruciatingly painful death. She barely heard his next words.

'We both need a breathing space. I have to know . . . Kate?' His hands shook with a fine tremor as he carefully placed the portrait on the bed behind them. He turned her to him, attempting to gather her close, but his movements were clumsy, and Kate shrank away from him, knowing she would not be able to bear the slightest hint of sympathy.

She was terrified that the frozen state enveloping her senses would thaw into the anguish she knew was lying in wait for her. Terrified she would break down and beg him to let her stay, on any terms, any conditions. He rose, to her relief moving away, but staring at her downbent head, his eyes reflected all the agony she was feeling, if she had only looked up. But she could not.

'I'll move out if you like,' he offered, his voice clipped with strain.

'No—I have to leave this place as much as . . .'

'As much as me,' he finished for her with an abrupt, humourless sound. 'There's no need to spare my feelings, Kate.

Not at this stage. Where were you planning to go?'

'I don't know—I hadn't thought beyond getting away.'

'Your parents?'

'No!' she cried emphatically, the thought rousing her from her apathy. 'I don't want them to know. Not yet. Mom would be round with chicken soup before I could draw breath!'

Greg sighed, perhaps at the reminder of happier days, but the bitter taste of defeat was breaking through his rigid control. 'How would you feel about going to Wales?'

'Wales?' She could not think; her brain was wrapped in cotton wool. He averted his gaze as she looked up blankly, and raked his fingers through his dark hair.

'I bought the bungalow from Sam.' His lips twisted with irony. 'It was going to be your Christmas present.' He breathed deeply. 'You seemed . . . happy there for a while?'

'I—yes, all right. That's fine.'

'You want to go now?'

'Yes!' She was very near breaking point.

He gave a curt nod. 'I'll bring the car round while you finish packing.' He paused at the door. 'Kate—if you don't want your parents to know, I'll have to spend some time with you. I won't get in your way,' he promised harshly when she did not reply.

Then he left.

The long weeks following their painful parting proved an enforced maturing process for Kate. It was, she discovered, still possible to function as a human being; to eat, to sleep—sometimes to exercise. Her body took control whenever her mind rebelled.

In the beginning, it was her pregnancy which saved her from falling apart. The knowledge that, whoever else would be missing from her life, a part of Greg would be with her for all time was a great consolation to her.

She discovered that long, lonely nights of sleeplessness were a small price to pay for those few precious months of believing that Greg was falling in love with her. Her own all-encompassing love for him transcended the hurt he had caused her. For she did still love him, wanted, with a hunger so gut-wrenchingly intense at times, to live in their invitingly warm home with Greg and their baby—the baby she was certain had been conceived the night she had finally admitted, if only to herself—that she loved him.

Long weeks of isolation gave her the opportunity to contemplate their relationship more thoroughly than ever before, and she was forced to the conclusion that she had no one to blame for her current predicament but herself.

Greg had warned her from the very start that love had no place in his life. It would have been the easiest thing in the world for him to lie to her as many men would have done given her whole-hearted response to his lovemaking. She had been all too ready to lap up any soft murmurings of love and devotion—and would consequently have been even more devastated now. But he had been honest, even as he schemed to force her capitulation.

She had self-righteously accused him of trying to change her into the sort of woman he would have preferred her to be, but hadn't she tried to force the same compromise from him? She had done her best to turn him into a warmer, more loving man. Surely each was as reprehensible as the other, each demanding something the other was simply not capable of providing.

Emotional detachment was as alien to Kate as emotional involvement was to Greg.

And that, of course, was why she had mentally fought him for the two years leading up to their marriage. She had felt incompetent to the challenge of living with such a man, of giving her heart to someone so self-sufficient. Her warm, loving nature had rebelled against laying herself open to the very rejection which had her scuttling away like a scared rabbit rather than face his pity or, worse—his sense of responsibility. Something she had not taken into account when she left, but which she should have known would negate a complete severance of their relationship.

The notion of a long-distance relationship had not entered her mind in all the emotional turmoil of their parting. Her only thought had been escape. But now, having faced her cowardice, she felt obliged to compromise for all their sakes—hers, Greg's and not least of all their child's.

If she could accept the only things he had promised

her—honesty, and fidelity, then there was a chance their marriage could survive this crisis in some shape or form. And, it had to be admitted, those two considerations, crucial to any relationship, were more than a lot of marriages possessed.

With this more maturely objective outlook, a certain serenity descended upon her, fuelled by the growing realisation that a new phase had begun.

Their journey to Wales had been completed in silence. Kate, exhausted by the preceding emotion-packed hours, slept heavily most of the way. Greg stayed a scant five minutes at the bungalow, checking that she had everything she needed for the night.

As he drove away, she stood motionless at the window, dry-eyed even as she knew he took her heart with him. Her misery cut too deep for tears. She slept the clock round, emerging groggily into the kitchen in the late afternoon in a muzzy search for coffee. She found a note.

Greg had returned while she slept. The fridge was stocked with fresh provisions. Arrangements had been made with the local doctor for her ante-natal care. A middle-aged woman, Mrs Vera Claybourne, had been hired to take care of the bungalow. A car would be delivered for her use the next day. A list of local telephone numbers was attached: hospital, doctor, fire service, central heating engineer, plumber, garage, the police. She was also instructed to telephone Greg at the apartment each evening.

At the time Kate could have, indeed did, scream, feeling that he was haunting her even from miles away, but she came to realise he would have been dogging her footsteps no matter what.

Their originally stilted phone conversations became guardedly friendly. Curt enquiries regarding her health were gradually transformed into ever-lengthening discussions about anything and everything. Greg talked about his work—the new contract Courtney's had received, his plans for a new factory in Northern Ireland. He spoke of Sam and Marie, of Kate's parents. Of how well her father's new business was doing. Of Toby Marchant's enforced transference to East Anglia. Kate in turn talked about her days: Vera's insistence on her drinking milk—which she hated, but Mrs Claybourne was, in her way, as formidable as Mrs Arthur. There was the craving she had developed for oranges and sardines—fortunately not at the same time! She told him of her tour of the local cottage hospital where she presumed her baby would be born.

They also began a series of long-distance chess games. After six weeks, their nightly chats were consuming more than an hour at a time—longer than they had ever spoken during the whole time they were together. The only taboo subject recognised by both parties was their future.

And slowly Kate found she might have lost a lover, but she was gaining a friend.

It was Christmas Eve before she saw him again, two months to the day after she had left. She had phoned him in a panic a couple of days earlier when the import of the date hit her. She had nothing prepared, but Greg calmly assured her that everything was in hand.

He arrived late on Christmas Eve. Kate was feeling incredibly confused at the thought of seeing him again. She was very conscious of how drastically her body had altered over the weeks since she had last seen him. As she had always been small-breasted it came as a distinct shock to look down one morning to find she had a very well-defined cleavage. She was now, in fact, bordering on the voluptuous! That alone would have been eminently acceptable, but the size of her belly had also increased dramatically, so much so that her doctor had sent her for a scan in the event that she might have been expecting twins, but only one baby had been determined.

But, more than her appearance, which had never really overly concerned her, she was very apprehensive of how Greg would treat her now he was aware that she was in love with him.

So it was with a measure of relief that she discovered Greg was not alone. He had brought her parents and brothers to stay for the holiday—quite a feat, considering her father's well-known reluctance to budge from his own fireside at Christmas time. Kate greeted them all with tearful hugs. It felt so good to be part of a family again.

She lifted shyly grateful eyes to Greg, who, after one comprehensively roaming look, pulled her gently towards him and bestowed a swift, hard kiss on her surprised mouth. Once her family were settled and the enquiries over health and the oohs and aahs over the luxurious appointments of the bungalow had taken place, Greg followed Kate into the kitchen to prepare refreshments.

'Your parents think I've been spending my weekends here,' he began warily as Kate discreetly drank in his appearance. He was looking tired, she thought—and he seemed to have lost weight. His face was leaner, his cheekbones prominent. His eyelids hooded his expression from her, but she sensed, with her deep instinctive knowledge of him, that he was as acutely miserable as herself. 'You did say you didn't want them to know about our—separation.'

'Yes, thank you. And thank you for bringing my family, Greg. I—I didn't realise how much I was missing them.'

'Even with the complications they present?' A familiar brow rose in sardonic enquiry. She looked at him blankly. 'The bedroom accommodation, Kate. Yes, precisely,' he added as her face flamed in comprehension—and expectation?

Of course they would have to share a room, she thought with a half-forgotten leap of the senses. Her parents' suspicions would be aroused immediately if Greg were to sleep elsewhere. They must already be wondering why Kate had moved to Wales. She gathered from her mother's phone calls that Greg had proffered explanations which seemed to have sufficed, though Kate did not probe too deeply. Her lashes lowered to hide the flash of hope she knew her eyes would reveal. Greg didn't seem too thrilled at the prospect.

'Well, it can't be helped,' she said woodenly, and fixed her sight on a point over his shoulder to await whatever taunting barbs he chose to throw her way.

'You're seeing the doctor regularly?' he asked curtly, his eyes moving restlessly over her expanding figure. Kate blinked at the change of subject. She had been certain Greg would derive great amusement from her predicament.

'I—er—well, I've only seen him twice, so far.' He frowned. 'There's no need for further check-ups yet,' she reassured him. 'Not until the last couple of months. Everything is fine. Really.' How absurd to feel shy under Greg's scrutiny!

'Pregnancy would appear to suit you, Kate,' he said finally, and picked up the laden tray. 'You're looking very—well,' he added, motioning for her to open the door.

They passed a surprisingly pleasant evening. After tea, Greg brought in a large Christmas tree from the trunk of his car, together with a box of decorations and an enormous pile of presents.

'Your mother helped me out,' he explained with a crooked smile at Kate's astounded face. And she *was* astounded. Did this mean Greg had actually asked her mother for a favour?

Inevitably, though, the evening drew to a close, and before she knew it Greg was closing the bedroom door behind them. The bedroom which had witnessed her initiation into love.

'Would you like to shower first?' he asked quietly.

'I—er—yes. If that's all right?' Kate could not meet his glance, remembering the showers they had shared while on honeymoon here. She kept her eyes fixed on the cream-coloured carpet.

'You have no need to worry, Kate,' he told her harshly, misreading her expression. 'I have no intention of taking advantage of the situation!'

Oh, if only you would, Kate thought longingly, but held her tongue. Any moves to re-establish their relationship had to come from Greg this time. Kate had learnt her lesson well.

She was lying still as a mouse on the extreme edge of the bed when Greg joined her. She tried to control her breathing so he would think her asleep, but she need not have bothered. He snapped off the light and lay on his side, his back towards her.

She sighed, absurdly disappointed by what seemed to be a firm rejection of her. She closed her eyes sadly, willing sleep to come and put her out of her misery, but a sudden fluttering in her stomach made her eyes snap open again. As always, the wonder of Greg's baby moving inside her filled her with a thrillingly possessive awe. She put her hand over the spot and felt again the as yet feeble tremors of life within her.

'What's the matter, Kate? Can't you sleep?' Greg asked gruffly, her movements, though slight, obviously disturbing him.

'Oh, Greg! Nothing's the matter. Feel!' Impulsively wanting to share the moment, she grabbed his hand and placed it over the mound of her stomach. 'It's our baby. Can you feel it?'

'Yes . . .' he muttered thickly, and jerked his head away as if he had been burnt.

'Greg . . .?'

'For heaven's sake, Kate! It's bad enough trying to sleep with you just lying there—but . . . Oh, to hell with good intentions!'

He pulled her to him roughly, kissing her with the dammed-up hunger of the past two months. There was no thought of denying him. She responded blindly, her hands roaming restlessly over his naked body, as his own hands discovered the altered contours of hers.

They moved together exquisitely. Never had Kate received such tenderness from him as they made poignantly ecstatic love.

And afterwards, Greg kissed away the tears she had been unable to stem. Tears comprised of so many things—the waste, the loneliness, the longing—the love.

'We'll work it out, Kate. I promise.'

Kate clung to that promise in the following weeks. Greg visited her at least once a fortnight, ostensibly to keep up appearances. But Kate knew he had never given a damn for other people's opinions. Sometimes he brought her family, sometimes Sam and Marie. And once he brought Terry, laying that particular ghost to rest for all time. Kate was grateful for Greg's intuitive understanding. She hated the thought of a rift appearing in the friendship she valued so highly. She was also pleased to see a friendship developing between the two outwardly disparate men.

This time around, she did not dwell on the idea of building a new relationship with Greg, simply accepted whatever came her way during their all too brief reconciliations. Their nightly telephone conversations spilled over to their meetings, tentatively at first, but deepening into an easy comfort in each other's company—until they retired to bed. There was no pretence of separate bedrooms. Their hunger for each other was undiminished.

The memory of those long nights of lovemaking kept Kate sane through the lonely days until Greg returned. At the very least, she had the consolation of knowing he still desired her. She had not the slightest fear that he was involved with anyone else. Their lovemaking was so very urgent, as if they were both terrified it would be their last contact. And gradually it became clear that Greg intended their marriage to stand.

Except that not once did he ask her to return to him.

If this long-distance relationship was all they would have, Kate was prepared to accept it. She had already learnt that pride was a cold bedfellow. She was even glad in many ways that Greg knew how she felt about him. But, as her time grew near, she grew ever more conscious of experiencing a state of suspended animation, of the need to know exactly what her future held.

'Nest building', Marie would have called it. Certainly the bungalow shone from Kate's constant cleaning. But how could she build a proper nest if she did not know where it was to be situated? She found it impossible to believe Greg was happy with the present arrangements, even though he did nothing to alter them. She had sensed his basic loneliness even at the height of their lovemaking. Her growing maternal instincts longed for the right to care for him, to check that he was eating and sleeping properly and not burying himself in work.

A breathing space, he had said. Surely nearly five months was long enough? The Greg she had married would have made up his mind in an instant, but this new, guardedly friendly Greg was obviously not so sure of himself. Kate sighed as a vicious kick to her ribcage reminded her of the baby due in the next two weeks. Would his or her arrival signal the end of this incessant waiting period? Or would it precipitate the end of her marriage? Even in her darkest moments she could not believe that.

She and Greg between them had created a new life, fusing them together in the most intimate way possible. Greg had to be part of her foreseeable future. Hadn't she once told him he accepted the consequences of his actions? No, there was no way he would ever turn his back on his child. And his wife? Whatever he decided about her, Kate knew she was now strong enough to accept. If only she knew what it was to be!

She admitted that part of this continual restlessness was caused by the fact that Greg had not been near her for a month. He had begun phoning her instead of the other way round. He was pretty busy, he had said. Solicitous as ever, but—busy. Kate could not help but feel a little neglected, especially as the baby had seemed to double in size since she had last seen her husband. Was that why he hadn't come? Because it was impossible for them to make love?

Which was why she found herself sitting staring at the phone one windy early April morning, willing the phone to ring—and knowing it wouldn't for at least another eleven hours. She gave a wistful sigh and made to move away, only to almost jump out of her skin a moment later when the ringing sounded throughout the emptiness of the bungalow.

CHAPTER ELEVEN

'GREG?' she whispered into the receiver, hardly daring to believe it could be him.

'Fraid not, princess,' came Terry's apologetic though cheery voice.

'Oh—hello.' She tried to inject a little more enthusiasm into her voice. 'What's got you out of bed this early—or should I say who?'

'I always thought pregnant ladies became sweet and placid,' Terry complained. 'I was merely wondering if you fancy some company today?' he added in a casual tone which didn't fool Kate for a moment. He was up to something. But that didn't matter. She was tired of her voluntary exile.

'Yes, please,' she agreed with fervent meaning.

'Right,' he sounded amused, 'I'll be with you for lunch.'

Kate put down the receiver slowly, a stray thought beginning to take root . . .

'My goodness, Kate, how you've grown!' Terry's eyes twinkled over her ever-expanding figure.

'The correct word is bloomed,' she corrected him with an indignant sniff. 'There's no need to remind me that I look like an elephant!'

She caught up on the news from the home front over lunch, and she made Terry laugh when she described the ante-natal classes she was attending. She waited until he had sipped the last of his coffee before dropping her bombshell.

'Are you very tired of driving today, Terry?' she asked with assumed casualness.

His head tilted to one side, taking careful note of the nervous way she was crumbling a bread roll between her fingers. 'You want to go for a drive this afternoon?' he asked gravely.

'I . . . no. That is . . . Yes, I . . . What I mean . . .' To his great

171

consternation, and her total surprise, she buried her face in her hands and burst into tears. Once started, she could not stop, despite his comforting arm around her shoulders and the soothing words he was uttering.

'Oh, love, you are in a mess, aren't you?'

Kate raised a blotchy face for him to wipe away her tears. 'I want to go home, Terry,' she sobbed. 'I hate it here—it's lonely. And I want Greg. And—and just look at me!' He did, very comprehensively, but that only caused her to cry harder. She struggled to her feet to go on a search for tissues. 'He doesn't want me any more, does he? I need to know, Terry. And—and he hasn't been near me for weeks!' She gave a sigh of utter misery. 'I can't blame him.' Her face threatened to crumble again. 'Who wants to be married to an elephant?'

'And a waddling elephant at that!' Terry agreed, deadpan. Fortunately it had the desired effect on Kate. A feeble giggle escaped her and her forlorn expression lightened a little. She hadn't realised until now just how very miserable she had been.

'Go and pack your bags, princess, and we'll be off.' He grinned down at her. Kate studied her nails very carefully.

'Actually, they're already packed.'

'Then what are we waiting for?' He offered her his arm. 'Your chariot awaits, ma'am.'

'I thought you'd come in the lorry, Terry. Didn't you have a load to deliver?' asked Kate as she clambered into his car. Terry did not answer until he was safely buckled in. He frowned thoughtfully.

'Yes. I'm delivering it now.'

'You're delivering it?' Kate stopped trying to stretch the seat-belt while she assimilated his statement. 'You expected to take me home?'

'Let's just say I was hoping to persuade you,' he answered quietly. 'Look, love, I really don't think that seat-belt will stretch any more. You'd better sit in the back seat.'

She shot him a sharp glance. Fortunately, he allowed not a glimmer of amusement at her predicament to show. She heaved herself out of the car and carefully lowered herself into the back seat.

'Pregnancy is so dignified, don't you think?' she muttered airily as he started the car. She waited until they were under way before asking the question burning in her mind. 'Did Greg ask you to come for me?' She waited with bated breath for his reply.

'Greg isn't asking anyone for anything these days. And he certainly wouldn't thank me for interfering.'

'Then why?'

'Because you're both behaving like a pair of bloody idiots!' His voice rose angrily, all the more forceful because Kate was not used to seeing him as anything other than amiable. 'You're stuck here in your ivory tower missing Greg like the devil, and Greg——' he took a deep breath. 'I've come to know him pretty well since you did your disappearing trick. I like him, princess. He's a good bloke. Now, I don't know what came between you—I don't need to know. Whatever it is it can't possibly be enough to keep you apart. He needs you, Kate. And with a bloke like Greg, that's really saying something. He's been on a few trips with me and Callum, lately. Did he tell you?'

'No,' Kate answered thoughtfully. 'To tell you the truth, I forgot all about the business. How's it going?'

'We're on our way to our first million!' He grinned. 'Seriously, we're doing better than I could have hoped, thanks to Greg. Though I must admit I was surprised when he asked Callum and me to train him for his HGV licence.'

'Greg asked you?'

'Hey, I didn't mind, love. That's what friends are for, eh?'

So Greg had changed to the extent that he could now ask favours—first of her mother and now Terry, of all people. It was certainly food for thought, but there was too much at stake for her to be able to trust Terry's reading of the situation. She had to find out for herself. Wasn't that why she had chosen to confront Greg now—together with her enormous belly, swollen ankles, and the various other indignities associated with pregnancy, rather than wait until after the baby's birth, when she might, once more, be an acceptable bedmate?

Terry cast her a glance through the medium of the mirror, taking careful note of her thoughtful features.

'Why don't you take a nap, love? Must be exhausting carrying all that extra weight around! Besides,' a tongue went firmly into his cheek at her affronted glare, 'that way, you don't get a chance to change your mind!'

And suddenly Kate did feel tired, tired of thinking, of analysing, of trying to determine her future with insufficient data. She closed her eyes against the passing scenery, not rousing from her deep sleep until the sound of raised voices pierced her mind.

She looked up dazedly, wiping the sleep from her eyes, and wondering why they had stopped. Her heart seemed to leap into her throat as she surveyed her surroundings.

She was home. Her home. The home she had seen and fallen in love with so many moons ago. But how different it looked now!

The overgrown front garden and surrounding orchard had been cleared and restoration work started. The house itself now stood proud and dignified in its new setting, a fresh coat of cream paint bringing it to sparkling life. All the windows had been replaced, and the curtains—even from this distance, Kate recognised them as the ones she had chosen from the pattern books she had devoured before leaving Greg.

The last she had seen of her designs, they were decorating the lounge carpet back at the apartment. But now—now they had been brought to life. She had not dared to ask Greg what he had done about the house, knowing she would not be able to bear the thought of it being demolished by someone who could not appreciate her precious white elephant.

Then her attention was diverted by the sound of Greg's furious voice.

'Just clear off, Terry—and keep your damned nose out of my affairs!'

Kate stretched, and immediately wished she hadn't. A lower back pain had been niggling away at her for most of the day and was now increased by the strain of sitting in one position for so long. Greg must have caught her movement out of the corner of his eye, because he turned suddenly and marched with angry strides to wrench open the car door.

'I'm sorry about this, Kate.' His voice was clipped—strained. He did not look directly at her, but Kate thirstily drank in every line of him. It was going to be all right—she knew that now. She had known the moment she saw the house.

Greg was looking tanned and fit. He was dressed in old jeans and a sweatshirt dappled by blobs of blue paint—the shade, if she was not mistaken, that she had chosen for one of the guest bathrooms. Kate had to lean heavily on his arm as she struggled inelegantly out of the car. The fresh-looking apple-green tent dress she had changed into for the journey was sadly creased and crumpled, but her eyes and cheeks glowed now that she was, at last, reunited with the man she loved. The man she had never stopped loving. The man, she now knew, who loved her.

'Terry had no right to subject you to this journey.' His grey eyes skimmed over her, then slid quickly to the ground.

'It was my idea, Greg,' she told him softly. His head shot up, his eyes alight with an emotion she had not dared to dream of.

'Why, Kate?' The words trembled from his lips, his whole stance rigid. Kate lifted her beautifully serene face to his, happiness breaking over her in waves.

'I wanted to come home. I've missed you so much.' Her voice shook on the last words, and Greg's control snapped.

'Oh, my love!' he breathed raggedly, gathering her as close as her bulging stomach would allow and raining kisses over her face and throat. Then he pulled back, his gaze moving restlessly over her every feature as if he could not believe she was finally here, where she belonged. In his arms.

Neither of them noticed Terry start up his car and steal away, a broad grin splitting his handsome face.

'I hate to sound prosaic, darling,' Kate pulled herself with great reluctance from Greg's tight hold, 'but if I don't get to a toilet soon . . .'

He threw back his head and laughed out loud, a rich deep, vibrantly happy sound. As they reached the threshold of their new home, he suddenly swung her high up into his arms, grinning down at her surprised yelp.

'I'm starting our marriage properly this time around!'

Kate gasped in astonishment when she saw the magnificent hall. It was exactly as she had planned it—oak panelling and a russet carpet which should have clashed horribly, but the immense proportions of the hall absorbed it superbly.

'Hey . . .' Greg tapped her on the shoulder. 'The toilet,

remember? The door on the right. I'll make us some tea.'

Kate joined him in the kitchen as he was pouring the tea. He looked more relaxed than she had ever seen him before—and she knew, in some way, she had been right in thinking his surroundings made a difference to his mood. Just as her impulsive decorating of their apartment bedroom had changed him subtly, their white elephant had wrought a miracle.

The kitchen too matched her plans down to the gaily patterned roller blinds. Greg, ever the practical man, had thought to add a laundry room. It was only sparsely furnished as yet, a small picnic table and a couple of stools—and Kate knew Greg had been awaiting her return before choosing furniture.

She sipped her tea gratefully, thirsty after the long journey, and stared out at the back garden, thoroughly transformed from the jungle she had first seen. Turf was stacked to one side ready to be laid, and all the borders were freshly dug. It would take years for the garden to become fully established, but the first mighty steps had been taken.

'I might have known you'd mess up all my plans! You've done nothing less since I first met you.' Greg pulled her back against him and a sigh of pure happiness escaped her as strong fingers kneaded her aching spine.

'I couldn't stand not knowing any more. I needed to know where to build my nest, and here you were building it for me.'

'Everything was supposed to be finished by the time Junior made an appearance. That's why I haven't been to see you this past month . . .'

Kate tilted her head to one side to rub her cheek against his hand.

'You meant to bring me here after the baby's birth?'

'Where else?' He stopped, suddenly unsure of himself. 'That is, if you . . .?'

Flattering in its way as it was, Kate could not bear to see this strong proud man she loved humbled before her. She turned in his arms, pressing quieting fingers to his lips. Her face was radiant.

'We're going to be so happy here, my darling.'

A spasm of pain passed over Greg's softened features as he pressed a reverent kiss in the palm held to his lips.

'Kate . . .' Her name was groaned on a sigh. 'Kate, I . . .'

Her hand moved to caress his lean cheek, longing to see the return of that incongruous dimple.

'Are the words so hard to say, Greg?'

'I've never said them before,' he said with stark simplicity. She smiled a little tremulously, a lone stray tear trickling down her cheek to be captured by his lips.

'I'm told—I'm told it comes easier with practice.'

'Kate.' His head lowered, as if he could not bear to look at her as he uttered the magical words. 'I love you, Kate. I love you so much it's tearing me apart!'

'Oh, Greg!' she whispered on a broken sob, the tears silently overflowing. 'I've waited so long to hear those words!'

'And you're going to make me wait even longer, is that it?' he questioned sharply, a tiny flicker of uncertainty clouding his eyes.

'I love you, Greg.' She reached up to trail her fingers down his cheek, rubbing her thumb over his lips. She groaned at the sensation evoked as he captured the pad of her thumb between his teeth. It seemed a little shameless in her so very pregnant state. But it was also an inevitable outcome of being near this man she loved so completely. 'I never stopped loving you, Greg. Don't you understand how impossible that would be?'

And their lips finally met in a lingeringly slumbrous kiss which conveyed more than words ever could.

'Why did you make me wait, Greg? You did love me when I left, didn't you?' It was not a question. She had realised that fact on first sight of their home. 'There was no need to go to all this trouble when mere words would have convinced me. You've never lied to me . . .'

'Haven't I?' He shook his head sadly. 'Kate, my darling Kate, I've been lying to you—to myself, all the way through this damned charade!'

He stepped back a pace, raising his fingers to bridge his nose, absently rubbing at the frown lines etched between his eyes.

'Sit down, Kate.' He brought their tea over to the picnic table and Kate perched as best she could on one of the stools.

'There were so many reasons why I let you go, Kate. They don't feel so valid now, but . . .' A faint smile touched his lips to offset the frown, though nothing could quench the warm glow Kate's unexpected arrival had brought to his eyes—eyes which never left his wife's face during his long-overdue narrative. He kept a firm hold of her hand throughout, and they both knew that soon, very soon, there would be no secrets left between them. 'You have to understand, love has never possessed the same connotations for me as it does for you . . .'

And the story unfolded of a young Yorkshire miner and his beautiful but resentful wife—resentful because she had been forced into marriage by Greg's premature conception. Of how Ben, as proud as only a Yorkshire miner—that toughest of breeds—can be, forgave his wife's infidelities time and time again, worshipping her, even as she stamped his pride into the dust.

'Can you imagine what it did to him? Going down the pit day after day wondering which of his colleagues had made it with his wife?'

Kate longed to interrupt him, to tell him she did not need explanations, but she forced herself to remain quiet, knowing that Greg had kept this old bitterness locked inside him for far too long.

'Every time she came back he forgave her—rewarded her, even. He was bringing in good money then, up until his accident. When he realised he was no good to her as a man any longer, he let her go.'

Unaware of the slow tears trickling down her face, Kate squeezed his hand hard in silent support.

'He cried that night—the night she left. I'd never seen him like that. He sobbed and sobbed—I couldn't reach him. Damn it!' He slammed his cup down with a crash. 'What the hell does a ten-year-old kid know about broken hearts? He never recovered. He was still in love with her the day he died.' Eyes bleak with anguished memories caught at Kate's heart with painful intensity. Greg's voice dropped to a whisper.

'I loved my father, Kate, but heaven help me, I despised him for that weakness which made him give up living. He was just an empty shell from then on.

'I've never forgotten that night he sobbed in my arms. I swore I would never allow any woman that power over me—and that neither would I ever put anyone else in that position.'

'Then that's why Marie . . . At our engagement party, she said how happy she was that you'd finally allowed someone like me to love you. I thought it strange at the time,' said Kate.

'I guess she knows me better than I thought. I practically lived with her and Sam after Dad died . . .'

'Your mother?' she prompted gently, as she had once before. This time, though, was different.

'She was quite happy with the arrangement, my love—and so was I. She'd never really been around long enough for me to miss her idea of motherhood.' And suddenly Greg laughed. 'I overheard her proposition Sam once, you know. He cut quite a figure in those days, and she was very beautiful—very exotic for those parts. He gave her the dressing-down of her life! I've loved that man ever since. Certainly there was no other man in the village able to resist her.'

'Ah, but he was in love with his Marie . . .'

He caught Kate's question before she could ask it. 'And why didn't I follow their example instead of my parents'?'

He was thoughtful for a moment. 'I always knew there was as much of my mother's character in me as my father's. I loved him—but I could still stand back and be appalled at the way he allowed her to treat him. I never really knew her well enough to care one way or the other. Even with you I could be objective—at first. Right up until I kissed you. Once I knew how good you felt in my arms . . .' he ran a thumb over the lush curve of her lips, 'well, things got pretty confusing from then on.

'You see, one thing was very clear to me from the start—I was totally the wrong sort of man for you. You were right about that—you said marriage to you meant sharing a life, remember?' Kate nodded. 'I didn't know how to share, Kate. Or even how to give. And I knew that you were close to falling in love with me . . . you're not very good at hiding your feelings, are you?' Kate could only ruefully agree with that judgement. 'It was a temptation, you know—it felt so good—but . . .'

'You didn't want me to suffer the way your father did,' she finished for him.

'I didn't do a very good job of protecting you, did I?'

'Hush, Greg!' she applied firm fingers to his lips. 'It doesn't matter—not now.'

But Greg was determined that all past ghosts in their relationship should be laid firmly to rest.

'Caroline was a last-ditch effort to keep me away from you, but it never stood a chance. The whole damned affair only lasted a month—if that, whatever she may have intimated to the contrary.'

'Oh!' Kate's eyes had begun to take on the green glow Caroline's name invariably produced, but Greg's assertion gave her pause. 'I thought it was a long-standing sort of thing. After all, you met her when you first moved here . . .'

'I can assure you, my first reactions to you were too overpowering for me to notice any signals she might have been sending my way!' he assured her with a dry intonation. 'I bumped into her—oh, about fifteen, sixteen months later. Kate . . .'

'Well, as long as you promise never ever to mention that name again . . .'

'I promise.' He raised his hands in a gesture of truce, only to lower them again immediately to frame her face lovingly. 'You're like a miracle to me, my darling. So warm—so giving. The first time I kissed you, I felt as if I'd truly found my home.'

Kate's eyes misted at the loving words so alien to him . . . until they registered. She sat up straighter in surprise, trying to ignore the uncomfortable sensations around her middle section. This was far more interesting!'

'Are you saying you've loved me since then?'

Greg sighed. 'Long before that, probably—I just didn't recognise the fact. You scared the hell out of me when I first set eyes on you. Yes, you did,' he persisted at her snort of disbelief. 'You looked up from your desk . . .' he tugged her hair loose from its restraining ponytail '. . . and these little wisps of hair were framing your face. And you were smiling so damned provocatively.'

'I was not!' she retorted indignantly. 'I was just being my natural charming self.' She pulled a face at him. 'And you looked down your arrogant nose and scared me half to death. I guess I knew then you were going to have a great impact on my life.'

'You too?' Greg smiled at her resigned nod. 'Well, that was the first of my plans you ruined. I'd decided to begin a new business venture once the Midlands Office was set up. As a matter of fact, that was the main reason for moving—the Midlands being an area of high unemployment . . .' It was then he noticed Kate's mouth was gaping open.

'How could you leave your own firm?' she squeaked.

'Very easily, Kate my love. Courtney's is so well oiled it practically runs itself. The challenge had gone out of it. Until I saw you . . . and thought I'd stick around for a while to see what developed.'

'Considering how expendable you thought you were, you certainly kept me busy! All those evening conferences . . .' Kate stopped abruptly, noticing a flicker of guilt pass over his face. 'They weren't necessary at all, were they?'

Greg shifted uncomfortably but finally confessed, 'I overheard you making a date . . .'

'Oh, you . . .!' Words failed her, but Greg breathed a sigh of relief at the teasing glint in her eyes—confident she could now forgive him anything. Which she would, now she had her life back.

'I hadn't been moulding you into the sort of woman I thought I needed for someone else to reap the rewards!' There was a logic about that she was rather afraid she understood. 'Anyway, rest assured the firm made tremendous profits last year from all those extra hours we put in.'

'You're outrageous!'

'And you wouldn't change.' Greg shook his head in mute wonder. 'I kept piling extra responsibilities on you, but you stayed the same sweetly vulnerable girl you'd always been—under that terrifying efficiency, of course.'

'Hah! Terrifying my foot! I was scared stiff you'd realise you'd made a big mistake promoting me, and I'd lose all that money. We needed it.'

'Mm, I know that now—but then I was too aware of the fact that I could hurt you badly. Kate, my love!' he cried out as a spasm of pain hit her. 'What is it?'

'I'm all right!' she protested. 'I just felt a bit weird . . .'

Greg picked her up as if she was a featherweight rather than a waddling elephant, and carried her upstairs into the master bedroom suite, laying her on the king-sized bed as if she were porcelain.

Kate looked around her with interest. This room was a facsimile of the one she had decorated at the apartment. All the furniture was the same—but there was one addition, hanging in pride of place on the wall facing the bed. Her portrait sketch of him.

'Dammit all! I knew you should never have made that journey!' he burst out, raking angry fingers through his hair. Kate reached up a hand to pull him to her.

'Are you saying you wished I hadn't come?' she teased.

'Lord, no!' He looked appalled at the thought. 'I don't think I could have stood this half-life much longer.' He stretched out beside her, cradling her head against his chest as he played with her hair. 'You can't imagine how often I've lain here wishing you were beside me again.' He nodded towards the portrait. 'I'd stare and stare at that picture, praying that the love you felt when you sketched it was too strong to die. And, when the uncertainty got too great. I'd drive hell for leather to Wales to see you. I nearly asked you to come back several times—but I knew it wasn't right to take you back to the apartment, and this place was uninhabitable until last week . . .'

He laid her back on the pillow, not giving her a chance to speak, but lowering his head to lips parted and waiting for his.

'Are you sure you're all right, love?' he asked worriedly a little while later.

'I am now,' she whispered happily, cuddling closer to him. 'It's just backache, mainly.'

'Here?'

'Mm. That's better!' She arched against his gently rubbing hand.

'Yeah—well, be a good girl and stop wriggling, will you? You know,' he murmured musingly after a while, 'that day I walked into your office to find you punching Toby Marchant on the jaw was the great turning point.'

'It was for me too,' Kate murmured drily.

'I'd waited so long for a break in that cool façade, I pounced the moment it cracked.'

'You certainly did!' she smiled, but Greg's face was set in more serious lines.

'One little taste and you took me over. I felt like a damned teenager again, losing control every time I came near you.'

'Hah! You couldn't prove it by me!' She snuggled further back against him. 'You were a master manipulator. I never knew what you'd do next.'

'Neither did I,' he complained bitterly. 'All I could think about was making love to you—being inside you. I was obsessed, Kate. I knew I was turning into a monster, but I couldn't stop. I've never needed anyone before—it's pretty scary.

'So—I started planning the best way to get on a more personal footing with you—you know, all nice and slow and easy. Then I was handed the perfect opportunity.'

'Dad!'

'Yes.' He sighed heavily. 'I don't know if you can believe this, but I would never have used that contract against your family. I was going to tell you how wrong you were when I thought it was the perfect way to stop you loving me.'

'I worked that out ages ago, love. Just before I admitted to myself that I was well and truly hooked on you,' Kate told him softly. 'It was something Terry said—about my being unable to marry for anything but love—and everything clicked into place. I grabbed at that contract as an excuse to give in.'

'It seems we owe a lot to Terry, one way or another.'

Kate had to smile at his disgusted expression. 'As Terry would say—that's what friends are for. Were you really jealous of him? I still can't quite believe that, you know.'

Greg shot her a dry look. 'Not of Terry, per se. Though I must admit there were moments . . . You were so comfortable with him, my love. I also knew he was much more your type than a cold bastard like me!'

'Hey!' she admonished him sharply. 'No one insults the man I love!'

He cleared his throat. 'Well, meeting him brought all my plans forward, until you messed them up again! I fully intended to make love to you that first night at the apartment . . .'

'Well, you could have,' she assured him.

'Dear heaven—I swear I will never know how I let you go that night! But if you'd seen your face—so full of panic and a sort of wonder . . .' He hugged her close in apology. 'I'd never much cared for anyone's feelings before. But you were so open, so honest, I felt I had to give you the opportunity to decide for yourself.'

Kate bristled a little indignantly at that. 'But I said no, Greg.'

His lips quirked in a purely masculine smile. 'You didn't really imagine I'd leave it there? Even as I was mouthing that damned proposition, I knew it would never be enough—for either of us. In my arrogance, I decided marriage was the answer—both to your need for commitment and as a salve to my conscience. But you came back with all those good sound reasons why we shouldn't get involved. You gave me some bad moments there, Kate. Not least of all because you were right.

'And then, of course, I found I'd underestimated that filthy temper of yours . . .' He ducked, protecting his face with his arms as she made a threatening gesture.

'Oh, Greg, I hated the way you could make me feel with one touch. It went against everything I believed in. I thought I was going mad . . . I suppose I was really. Mad about you!'

For which piece of honesty Kate was well rewarded.

'You remember that time you were ill?'

She nodded. 'Yes. That was the first time I thought marriage to you might not be too bad after all. You looked after me so nicely.'

'Those were my orders,' he reminded her of Alissa's strictures. 'But that was the time I began to admit what was happening to me. I sat with you while you slept and this little voice kept whispering in my ear that it would be safe to love you . . .'

'But you didn't know if it was safe for me to love you?' she hazarded, strangely loving him more for his protective attitude towards her, despite the pain it had caused her.

'I was so torn, Kate. Nothing has ever lasted in my life—the one thing that had always challenged me was building the firm, but even that had begun to pall. When your parents walked in on us, I persuaded myself it was better that way—that if I could stop you getting too close, we could both walk away with minimal scars when it was over. But I hadn't taken into account your determination to do the opposite. When you told me on our wedding night that I would have to take from you, I realised how empty my victory was.'

'So you made sure I started giving?' she said drily.

'But you didn't really——Oh yes, you were very sweetly responsive, gloriously so, in fact—but I began to long for you to take the initiative. That night after I'd hurt my knee . . .'

Kate's eyes lowered demurely. 'I'd just admitted I loved you—it seemed the right thing to do at the time.'

'And it became my most treasured memory.' His lips curved reminiscently, his voice becoming a husky groan. 'Oh, Kate! I thought we'd reached the heights before,' his voice shook with remembered passion, the emotion darkening his eyes all that Kate had ever desired. 'You were so shy—and so damned sexy. I could feel you blushing all the time . . .' He grinned in delight as a new blush made an inevitable appearance. 'I knew then you loved me. You couldn't possibly have behaved so . . .'

'Wantonly?' Kate suggested, green eyes dancing.

'Mmm, that will do,' he smiled lovingly. 'I'd suspected it the day before—when I saw how you'd decorated our room. It was as if you were telling me you'd be with me forever.' He spread his hands wide. 'I was lost, my love. I was such a novice. You seemed content to let things drift, so I went along with it—terrified to rock the boat. I don't know even now how I stopped myself blurting it out when you told me about the baby. I was so relieved—I thought, that's it! She'll never leave me now . . . And then you found this place for us.' He leaned over her to frame her face with shaking fingers. 'I felt the same about it as you. As soon as you drew those sketches showing what it could be like. And I was petrified! You were tying chains around me so securely—your sweet self, our child, this place. I'd never imagined myself a family man. But I had this dreadful vision of everything being snatched away from me . . .' His hold on her tightened convulsively. 'It had happened so many times with my mother—she'd come back from one of her jaunts and everything would be sweetness and light for a while, then wham! Our lives would fall apart again.

'I wanted to wrap you in cotton wool—instead of which you

were tearing around like a mad thing—and when you declared your intention of doing some of the decorating yourself . . .' his brows lowered. 'I thought if you were to lose the baby then I'd lose my hold on you. And instead I had to throw you away myself.' He sighed with bitter regret. Kate opened her mouth to tell him to stop torturing himself this way, but said nothing, knowing all the bitterness had to be removed from his system before their new life could begin.

'I wish I could make you understand, Kate. When I saw you in Terry's arms, heard those words, I saw red. I didn't know how to handle vulnerability, but I think I must have gone a little mad. I locked myself in the office and paced the floor all morning. The firm—everything I'd spent my life working to achieve could have gone to the devil—but losing you . . .' He shuddered.

'Then I got angry—furious! I was damned if I was going to allow you to walk out of my life. So I called . . .' he stopped as he felt her stiffen warningly '. . . that woman. I thought I could make you suffer a little of the jealous hell I was going through. I nearly called it off when I saw how ill you looked, but those words kept going through my mind . . .

'When I saw that sketch and realised what I'd thrown away because of my own inability to trust in your love . . .' His voice broke and he laid his head on Kate's soft breasts.

She held him to her tightly. 'I wanted to show you that my love for you was as permanent as that for my family.'

'I know,' he sighed, and raised his head, still tormented. 'You looked as—broken as my father had the day my mother finally left. That's the main reason I didn't tell you then. I had to be certain I could be the sort of man who could share his life . . . You wouldn't have left me for a moment if you'd known the truth, would you?'

She did not need to think. 'No.'

'I needed this time to prove my love in the same way you had. One half of me kept saying you were better off without me—all I ever seemed to do was cause you pain. And I guess I needed to know what hell it was to live without you.

'I left you alone for as long as I could stand. But when your parents suggested staying with you over Christmas I jumped at the chance. I didn't know what to think when I saw you again—you were so beautiful, and so cool. You were obviously managing very well without me. I fully intended to leave you alone, but you touched me, and I was lost—again.' A sensuous smile crept over his face. 'I do hope you're going to make a habit of seducing me, Mrs Courtney!'

'You conceited . . .!'

'Oh, Kate!' he hugged her close. 'Those stolen weekends with you kept me sane! They gave me hope that all was not lost.'

'Same here,' she agreed ruefully. 'I could no more resist you than . . . control my temper!'

'Well, that augurs well for the future—I think!' he teased.

'Greg?' she asked some blissful moments later. 'How did you get the house done so quickly?'

'I finally got around to asking a few favours. Marie and your mother acted on your designs . . .'

'Oh, yes, that reminds me. What did you tell them about our separation?'

'The truth!' Kate gasped. 'More or less, anyway,' he continued. 'At first I spun them a yarn about not wanting you to tire yourself out doing the house up—but your mother saw through that straight away. She came round to the apartment determined to get to the bottom of it.'

'Oh dear!' groaned Kate, even more so when he added:

'I was drunk! Quite a woman, your mother.' Kate nodded. Lecture number six, she decided. She was wrong.

'She gave me hell! Until she saw that sketch, then she said, very quietly, "Do you love my daughter, Gregory?" And I said, "Yes, quite desperately." Then she nodded and said, "Then I trust you will put matters right." And she's never mentioned it again!' Greg sounded quite bewildered, but Kate understood.

'That's quite a compliment, you know. She wouldn't allow just anyone to hurt me!' The laughter in her voice took the sting out of the words, but Greg looked at her with something approaching awe.

'I always wondered what it would be like to be part of a loving family. I guess—I guess I'm finally getting to know. Oh, it feels good, Kate!'

'I know. I wish I could have known your father,' she said

wistfully.

'You've given him back to me, Kate, as the strong, proud man he really was. You've taught me that love—real love—strengthens, not weakens. Can you imagine the strength of character he must have had to send my mother away at the time he needed her most?'

'As you had the strength to send me away, my darling.'

He showed her over the house some time later. The top floor had yet to be touched, but Kate found herself delighted by the nursery Greg had decorated entirely alone.

'I know you'd decided on this as a dressing-room, but I thought it better to have the baby next to us.' His eyes sought her approval, which was readily given. The room was decorated in brightly patterned wallpaper, two huge mobiles hanging from the ceiling. He had also purchased a crib and low chair and a mountain of baby clothes—everything Kate had been too self-absorbed to think about.

'You don't mind the changed wallpaper? The books I read said bright colours were stimulating . . .' Greg held himself with great restraint as Kate succumbed to a fit of the giggles. 'Yes, well, it helped to pass the time.'

She threw her arms about his neck, hugging him fiercely.

'Oh, Greg! It's not so bad—loving me, is it?'

'It's been hell!' he groaned in a strangled voice. 'But now . . .' he took a deep breath and disentangled himself, 'to tell you the truth, it still scares the hell out of me, darling. Talk about hostages to fortune! I can't promise you sweetness and light all the way, love. I can't change my basic nature at this late stage . . .'

'I'm not exactly an angel to live with myself, Greg. In fact I'm told I have a very mean right hook.' Her eyes danced with mischief. 'At least when you start snarling at me again, I know it will be with love.'

'You can bet on it! Kate? How would you feel if I were to go and work with your father and Terry?'

She looked up in surprise. 'You were serious about leaving Courtney's to fend for itself?'

'I can still hold a watching brief—but I'd forgotten how good it was to get back to basics. How satisfying it is to build something from scratch.' He looked around him. 'I've enjoyed working on this place.'

'Mm. I'm told there are many advantages to men who work with their hands!'

He growled and kissed her fiercely.

'How long is this baby going to take, my love? I'm not sure of my ability to lie beside you all night without making love to you.'

Kate's tongue appeared to moisten suddenly dry lips. She knew she could put off telling him no longer.

'I don't think you have to face that problem just yet, darling. I won't be here tonight.'

Greg paled. 'Kate, you can't leave now . . .'

'No, Greg . . . I mean, I'll be spending tonight at the hospital.' His relief was short-lived as the implication hit him. 'Don't worry, love,' Kate reassured him with amazing calm. 'We've got hours yet.' She took his hand as they descended the stairs. 'And I could murder a bacon sandwich!'

Greg looked sick. 'How can you think of your stomach at a time like this?'

Then they burst out laughing at the unintentional pun, dispelling the panic.

CHAPTER TWELVE

'DAMMIT, Greg, I do not need a painkiller! I've spent months learning these breathing exercises so I wouldn't need an anaesthetic——Just leave me alone!' Kate broke off as another contraction took her over.

Greg muttered angrily as her face contorted with a spasm of pain.

He still managed to look completely dignified and authoritative even in the ridiculous cap and gown the midwife had insisted he wear, Kate thought resentfully as the midwife examined her yet again.

'Yes, I thought so,' the young woman murmured calmly. 'Take no notice of the bad temper, Mr Courtney,' she added with a flirtatious wink Greg did not even notice. 'It means the serious stuff is about to begin. Will you be staying for the birth?' Merry blue eyes twinkled at his sudden pallor.

Greg turned to Kate, his mouth dry.

'Do you want me to stay, darling?' he asked huskily.

'I'm scared, Greg.' Anxious green eyes stared a little wildly into his. Greg smiled at the midwife, once more in full control. His wife needed him.

'I'm staying.'

And it was Greg who, an hour later, placed their son in Kate's arms.

'Will you be naming him after your husband, Mrs Courtney?' the midwife asked.

Kate looked down at the tiny head cradled in her arms, at the little fingers curled around her thumb, at the already hungry mouth suckling at her breast.

'No,' she murmured. 'The next one, perhaps. But our firstborn will be named after a very special—loving man.' She looked up into Greg's unsmiling face. Her husband, her lover, the father of her child—and her best friend.

'With your agreement, my love, I'd like to call him Ben.'

'Did I ever tell you, my darling, just how very beautiful you are?' Greg's voice was hoarse with emotion as he looked deeply into his wife's loving face, not even seeing the red blotches from the strain of childbirth, but the woman he would love and cherish for the rest of his life.

'I'll go and get you both some tea,' the midwife announced.

They did not hear her.

'Do you think I stand any chance of catching a man like that?' the midwife asked the matronly ward maid with a sigh. 'He's a dreamboat!'

'Well, one thing's for sure, dearie,' the ward maid snapped, not without a touch of envy herself. 'You stand no chance with that one. Acting like a pair of soppy teenagers, they are.' She sniffed, and added with satisfaction, 'That won't last, you mark my words!'

But it did.